KEPT
WOMAN

By

A. R. Boyd

KEPT WOMAN

by

A. R. Boyd

Published by Hacienda Publications

Visit our website at www.haciendapublications.com

First Printing: May 2015

Cover Designed by M2 Magic Media

Table of Contents

INTRODUCTION

"There's no greater agony than bearing an untold story inside you."
Maya Angelou [1]

My story is born of pain. It's the kind of pain that reaches deep down inside you, and pulls up something pure and real. This kind of pain changes the course of things, and forces us to shift and re-evaluate who we are, and what's really important. At first sight, my story seems to be an unusual adventure of drug smuggling and corruption, prison stints and deportation. But, after further inspection you'll discover that it's really a love story unveiling passion and commitment, abandonment and betrayal, spanning over twenty precious years of my life.

For you die-heart love story fans, let me warn you. This story doesn't have the usual happy-ever-after ending. As a matter of fact, it doesn't have an ending at all. The last chords of my love song have yet to be written. Until the outcome, my hope is that you'll become immersed in my journey and hope for the same ending that I desire, to be reunited with my sweet, Hermes.

I'm writing this story, because I have to get it out of me before it drives me mad. Perhaps by sharing it with you healing may come, not only for me, but also for You. We all have wounds from a life that inflicts us with pain. If you haven't experienced it keep living, and your pain will come. No one is exempt. The good thing is, even though it hurts, pain can purify and burn off the trivial, foolish things in us. If we let it, pain can enrich us and make us strong thus, blessing us.

It helps me to know that I'm not on this journey alone. We are all fellow travelers helping each other to find our way. My hope is that we all discover the rainbow at the end of each of our trials, and that we release the love in us by sharing our journey with others. With this work, I share my journey with you, in love. Read and be blessed.

The Storyteller is clever and masterful,
and has already decided exactly what
he wants you to believe.

The Storyteller has the power to make people feel good
or bad about themselves.

The Storyteller has the power to make people feel strong
or weak, ugly or beautiful, confident or defeated.

Sista Soulja [2]

KEPT WOMAN

by

A. R. Boyd

Acknowledgements

There are too many people to thank for all of their love and support through the years.

I will keep it simple and Thank God!

KEPT WOMAN

Based on a true story.

(Names have been changed for the sake of anonymity.)

Chapter One
"The Melody Born"
"Joy and Pain... Like Sunshine and Rain"
Frankie Beverly and Maze [3]

My heart is broken. As I sit in my mother's home holding conversation and pretending that I'm in the moment, the truth is my heart and soul are in the Dominican Republic with Hermes. Every day I go through the motions. I work, socialize, eat and sleep, but there's clearly something missing, a hollowness inside that keeps me from feeling alive. My mind is racing, but when it slows down for just a moment I realize that I'm in a numb state of mourning, because I desperately miss my love and my soul mate, my sweet Hermes!

I remember every detail of the day I met him. He stepped through the door of my small walk-up apartment on Cromwell Street in Cleveland, Ohio, so handsome with dark curly hair. His stride was powerful with an unmistakable air of authority. Hermes's rich, mocha eyes scanned my apartment, then transfixed on me and I was held in my space, barely able to breath. From the moment Hermes walked into my apartment that warm, summer morning, I was totally attracted to him. I found out later that he was also attracted to me. I was surprised, because it looked like he had an air of indifference towards me. He told me later that he was just playing it cool, and sizing me up. He didn't want to lead me on in case he didn't like what he saw. That was just like him, to be all in or all out, never straddling the fence. He was, and still is an incredible man and I can honestly say that from the time I met Hermes everything in my life has been measured by, before I met him, to after. Hermes changed my life forever and I can never go back to being the person that I was.

I'm in a shattered place and it's not by chance that I arrived here. I believe that each of us sings a silent melody that seeks those whose melodies harmonize with our own. With that said, in order to understand how I got to this place we've got to go back to the beginning, to the place were the first notes of my melody were being composed.

First Born

My life started with trouble. I was a breech baby; born feet first and they usually say that breach babies grow up to be a little crazy. I don't know if that's true, but I've certainly experienced some crazy things. My mother was only seventeen and only God could have gotten us through what I was told, was a horribly painful experience. No one could have predicted it, but I now know that the conditions surrounding my birth were a sign that turbulent times were ahead for me, and my mother.

Growing up, my mother was a very studious person. Even though she was smart with a penchant for numbers, she was also a popular cheerleader with a very bubbly personality. She had it all and it's no wonder that in her senior year in high school she was voted most likely to succeed. My mother was definitely poised for success, that is, before she met my father.

Dad was a very mild mannered quiet man, a trait I believe he inherited from his mother Doris, who I call Grammy. My father loved baseball and spent most of his time on the baseball diamond. He had his sights on a professional baseball career and he was definitely good enough to make it happen.

Not only was my father gifted with baseball, he was also very fashion conscious. He was a sharp dresser, sporting the trendiest bell bottomed pants and stacked shoes. I was told that my father also had one of the best Afros around! He loved Jimi Hendrix and since Jimi was known for his fringed vest and guitar, my father also wore a fringed vest and had a guitar. When he wasn't playing baseball he would take his guitar and go to a corner of the house to practice playing Jimi Hendrix's riffs. He was pretty good, but he was definitely no Jimi Hendrix.

My mom and dad would sit for hours listening to music, and do really cool hand dancing. Back in the day hand dancing was common. People would sit around for hours and trip out on drugs and alcohol, using their hands to dance to the music. There was a popular female heroin on television. She would take the first two fingers of each hand and run them over her eyes like a mask. That move became legendary, and my mother and all her female friends would incorporate it into their hand dances. It was considered sexy and chic and it's lasted the test of time, because people still do it today.

My father drew a lot of attention because he drove a convertible Cadillac, and he kept it clean as a whistle! It's no surprise that he swept my mother off her feet and soon after they started dating my mother got pregnant with me. Even though they weren't mature or established enough to get married the story goes that my Grandmother forced them to the altar, although she vehemently denies it. One thing's for sure, back then you didn't raise a baby by yourself, especially if the father was available and willing to marry you. So, my mom and dad were married young without having an opportunity to experience life. My mother resented giving up her dreams to become a married woman with child, but she surrendered and settled down with my father.

As time went on, my mother started to notice that my father had issues. First, he was extremely jealous. He would watch my mother like a hawk and make note of every man that looked her way. Even after getting married and having me, my mother looked good and my father made sure that no other man would pull her away from him. That was a big annoyance for my mother and they argued constantly about my father's suspicions, and his attempts to control her. That's something I can relate to and I'm sure some of you can too.

One of the major issues that my father had was his love for strong alcohol and hash. He spent way too much time getting high. My father would drink and smoke all day and he encouraged my mother to do the same. She was never a drinker or a smoker and didn't know anything about getting high, but my father was insistent that she tried it. Almost everyday he would give her a little alcohol to drink, and teach her how to pull on a joint. In time, she started to get the hang of it, and even started to enjoy it. Once that happened, the drugs and alcohol became a major part of their lives and they both got high every day.

My father spent way too much time on the baseball diamond. Instead of going to class and keeping up with his assignments, he would skip class and spend all day playing baseball. He had an exceptional talent, a real gift, and the big leagues started to take note of it. When my father was still in school major league teams scouted him and during his last year in high school he was actually signed by the Pittsburgh Pirates! That would have been an incredible achievement for any man, but it was earth shattering for my father, because he was just a teenager in high school! He had done what few men his age had ever done and my entire family celebrated his success!

For a while, my father basked in his great fortune. But as fate would have it, the winds of change blew into his life. There's a passage in the Bible that basically says that, 'Once sin has done its complete work in you, destruction comes'. That's not the exact wording, but that's the essence of it and in my father's case, it was true. Even though he worked hard to perfect his baseball skills, he paid little to no attention to his education. The joke was that he skipped school so much, that his teachers forgot his name. It was an exaggeration, but my dad really did drop the ball and as a result, he didn't graduate on time. Fulfilling his educational requirements was one of the conditions of his contract with the Pirates, so they rescinded their offer to join the team. My dad went from being on top of the world to being dashed on the rocks and the devastation was great, not only for him, but for us too.

I really believe that my father has never recovered from the deep shame and disappointment. As the years passed he secured really good jobs, but he would never keep them. He was a spoiled brat who only wanted to play baseball, but the loss of his contract took the wind out of his sails and he was never able to secure another one.

I was with my father all the time. I knew that he loved me and I was totally fascinated by him. He was a quiet man, and really devoted to his family. He never ran the streets or neglected his family. My father was organized and well dressed and I wanted to be just like him. I learned cleanliness, organization and fashion sense from my father, and to this day I love having everything in order. I don't have OCD, but I do like my house, my car and everything to be neat, clean and organized.

My childhood was kind of strange. Even though I had two parents that lived daily with the pain of their broken dreams and disappointments, I still had a lot of support. I lived in a two-family home with my mother, father, grandmother, and great grandmother. I also had a host of aunts, uncles, great aunts and great uncles who all made sure I had everything that I needed. I was the first child born in my family in a long time, but I was also a very sick child. I suffered with severe asthma and had regular asthma attacks. They should have given me a special room at the Cleveland Clinic, because I practically lived there. I would be routinely rushed to the clinic unable to breath and they would admit me, keeping me there for days. During these episodes, my mom would spend the night with me on a cot. My dad would get upset, because she wasn't at home with him. Aside from his issues with my mother staying with me at the hospital, my dad adored me, as did my entire family and because of my health condition they were also overly protective of me.

I didn't think that I was spoiled, because I didn't believe that everything revolved around me. My cousin who lived across the street had a different opinion. He would come over my house to play and he would always say, "Cynthia you are so selfish! You don't share!" I don't remember being like that, but considering the circumstances of my life, it could be true.

My cousin really resented me. It could be because I was so doted on by my family or because he really believed that I was spoiled. Either way, it came to a head one day when I was real young. I was hanging out and playing with my cousin at his house. It was nice, with a large sixteen-step staircase that we played on all the time. This particular day, I was at the top of the stairs getting ready to slide down the banister, when my cousin came up behind me and pushed me down the stairs! It happened so fast that I didn't have time to grab a banister. I just went tumbling, head first, down the stairs. At first, I didn't realize what had happened until I looked up and saw my cousin looking down at me with a sly, half smile. I couldn't believe it. How could he do that to me knowing how sickly I was? From that point on, to say that my cousin resented me was clearly an understatement. He apparently wanted me dead! You have to hate someone to push them down the stairs. To this day he maintains that I dared him to do it, so he did. I don't remember that, but even if I did he should have declined the invitation. He really could have killed me.

Well anyway, after I fell I started screaming and calling for my parents!

"Ah!!! I screamed at the top my lungs! "Help me somebody! Please!!!" My cousin just stood at the top of the stairs watching me scream. He never made a move to help me. He had this strange look on his face, like he was looking at a mutated bird or something. I think he was shocked that he actually did it. He probably had been thinking about it for a long time. Who knows, he might have been standing at the top of the stairs wishing that I would stop screaming, and die. I didn't know for sure, but he looked really scary and I knew I had to get some help, and quick!

Finally, my parents came running and found me at the bottom of the stairs, bleeding. I thought my mother was going to faint.

"Oh, my God! My baby! My baby!" she kept screaming over and over again!

My dad yelled, "Back up! Don't move her! She might have broken her back!"

That's all mother needed to hear. She fell back on the stairs like a big fist had just hit her square in the chest. It was too much for her. I started to forget about my fall, because watching them yelling and running around was so entertaining. My grandmother, grandfather, great grandmother, aunt and uncle, all came running and for a while, it was mass confusion.

My grandmother, who was always the voice of reason calmly asked, "Did anybody call the ambulance?" Everybody stopped and looked at each other. Nobody had thought of that.

"Stop gawking and call the ambulance, for Christ's sake!" my grandmother said with disgust.

My aunt, who lived there, went to the living room and called the ambulance. While we were waiting, everybody one by one started to notice that my cousin was standing at the top of the stairs. By now, his face was pale as a ghost! He realized how serious the situation was, and he was terrified.

I lifted up my head and looked him dead in the eyes and I said, "He pushed me on purpose."

The blood rushed to my father's face, and he was red as a beet. He went charging up the stairs after my cousin, who tried to run and lock himself in the bedroom. My father caught him just in time, and he started whooping his tail like he was beating an African drum!

He yelled, "So you like to push little girls down stairs, do you? You tried to kill your cousin? Well, I'm going to kill you!" and he pulled the belt off of his pants, and started beating him for real!

I was so glad that I could have jumped up and started dancing. My aunt and uncle ran up the stairs and tried to pull my father off of their son.

My aunt was yelling, "My son wouldn't do that. He wouldn't try to kill his cousin!"

My uncle finally wrestled my father off of my cousin and yelled, "How you know Cynthia ain't lying?"

That's all my father needed to hear. He dived on my uncle and the two of them started wresting on the floor. My aunt and cousin jumped out of the way, screaming for help, but there was no one to help them. My grandmother, grandfather and great grandmother were too old, and my mother was lying on the floor about to pass out. Fortunately, we heard the sirens screeching and everyone stopped to run outside and guide the ambulance to the house.

The driver parked at the curb and two paramedics jumped out, opened up the back of the ambulance, and pulled out a stretcher. They pushed everyone aside and ran in the house. They spotted me through the chaos, and kneeled down next to me. One of paramedics asked me questions about where it hurt, but I couldn't tell him, because I really didn't feel any pain. They strapped me on the stretcher and took me to the ambulance. I was excited, because I had never been in an ambulance before. I had been to the hospital many times with my asthma attacks, but my mother would always drive me to the hospital.

As they took off and the sirens started sounding, I was smiling from ear to ear. It was so much fun. I heard later that you would have thought it was a funeral procession, because all of my relatives followed in their cars.

When I got to the hospital they bandaged up a few small scrapes, but other than that, there was nothing wrong with me. Everyone was shocked that I didn't break any bones and so was I. While they waited for me to be treated, I was told that there was a huge argument in the waiting room. The big question was, "Whose fault was it?" I was the golden sweet child that could do no wrong, so everyone was on my side except for my aunt and uncle. Of course, they sided with their son. Things started heating up again and if the security guard had not been there, my father and uncle would have come to blows again.

After the doctor released me, my parents hugged and kissed on me and I felt so much love from them that day. When I look at how everything has turned out for them, it makes me so sad. But, we'll deal with that later. For now, I went home and all the neighbors came over to see how I was doing. They all agreed that my cousin had an evil spirit. He was jealous of me and it should be no surprise that after the incident, I spent little to no time with him and that was just fine by him.

My mother spent a lot of time teaching me and instilling in me everything that she wanted to do with her own life. She went to Cleveland State University for Accounting, but didn't finish. I became an accountant and graduated from Cleveland State University. She played the flute and I played the flute. She was a very social person that helped other people and likewise, I was friendly and helpful. I idealized my mother and watched her like a hawk, mimicking everything she did. If she had to leave me for any length of time, I would have full-blown panic attacks and she was the only one that could bring me out of it. I always said that if I had children, I would treat them the way my mother treated me. She was a good mother and I was very dependent on her.

Who Does That?

As I said before, my childhood was strange. On the surface everything looked good. I had a strong, close family, so I had a lot of support. On the other hand, there was a dark side and I got my first glimpse of it at the age of three. One seemingly normal afternoon I walked into the kitchen and saw my father cooking something in a small bowl.

"What's that?" I asked, in my small, baby voice? He looked up, smiled and casually replied, "Hash."

Now, if you don't know, let me tell you. Hash is a strong form of marijuana and my father was cooking and smoking it right in the kitchen, in front of me. Even though I was only three years old, I can still remember every detail. It's almost as if something in me knew at the age of three, that what I was witnessing was not normal, and certainly not appropriate. When I look back on it, I believe I was witnessing the start of my father's drug addiction. The fact that he had no conscious about telling me he was cooking hash in our kitchen, showed just how much of a hold it had on him. No parent in their right mind would share drug details with a three-year old. I don't know if anyone in the family knew it, but my father was in trouble.

Dad started getting high at an early age, but my mother had never used drugs. He introduced her to the drug culture and by the time I was three years old, the drugs had a firm hold on both of them. The weird thing is, I don't recall anyone else in the house knowing about it. I don't know when it started to overtake them, but I believe that by the time I was three years old, the drugs had a firm hold on them. Maybe they did and just didn't discuss it around me. I don't know, but what they didn't know was that I already knew about it, and was all up in the middle of it.

From that point on, my parents got high around me all the time. They even took me with them to get high with friends. We would arrive at a house full of people smoking dope. Everyone would speak to me and treat me really nice, but I thought it strange that no one realized it was wrong to get high in front of me. Even though nobody gave me a direct hit, I'm sure that at some point I got a "contact", meaning, I inhaled some of the smoke. You can't be in a room full of hash smokers, and not be affected by it. If I was high, I didn't know it and I don't recall my parents ever talking to me about it. For them, our little smoking excursions were as normal as taking me to a friend's house for dinner, but I always knew it was wrong. I don't know how I knew. I just knew. Perhaps my parents were part of that movement that believed that since hash was a plant, it was natural, safe and even healthy. I don't know, but in my parent's case, it was definitely not beneficial.

School Days

While all this 'getting high' was going on, it was time for me to start Kindergarten. My birthday is in October, so I turned five after the August cut-off for admission therefore, I was not permitted to start Kindergarten. My mom was determined to get me into school so she fought and stayed in the face of the school administrators. She eventually wore them down and they allowed me to take tests to see if I was intelligent enough, and mature enough to start Kindergarten. I was a very smart kid and I passed all their tests with flying colors. Finally and reluctantly, the administrators gave me permission to attend Kindergarten at the St. Agatha St. Aloysius Catholic School. Even though my test scores were very high the administrators didn't think I would do well. They could tell I had issues, because I acted a little strange. Who knows? I might have had a 'buzz'. Whatever the case, I'm sure that no one would have guessed that I had a 'contact' from being around hash all the time. Either way, I surprised them all and actually did very well. I stayed at the St. Agatha St. Aloysius Catholic School until the eighth grade.

As far back as I remember, I was taught that there was a God. Perhaps going to Catholic schools most of my childhood reinforced that belief. In school we were taught about the cross and praying in the name of the Father, The Son and the Holy Spirit, as well as the Lord's Prayer. It was my attendance in Catholic schools that kindled my belief in God, Jesus, and his resurrection. In school, we always prayed in the morning before classes started. We also attended Mass a couple of times a week. My belief in God started there and I firmly believe that God had saved my life many times during my childhood and I must say, I love him for that.

When I was ten, I met the friend that remains my best friend today, Sidney and I liked her instantly. I think she intrigued me. I don't know why, maybe because she was so quiet. I was shocked when I found out Sidney had heart disease, the same kind as the woman in the movie,

Beaches. I think that intrigued me even more. Maybe since I grew up a sickly child, I was better able to empathize with her. Whatever the reason, Sidney and I were tight! We dressed alike and if Sidney didn't go to school, I didn't go. It was a great friendship and I treated her like the sister I never had.

At sixteen everything changed, because Sidney got pregnant! I was shocked, because I didn't even know she was dating. I was hurt too, because I thought Sidney and I were close, and shared everything with each other. I guess some things are too deep to share with your friends, especially me since I wasn't having sex. Maybe that's why she didn't tell me. I don't know why, but I decided to get over it, and continue being her friend. My mom was upset too and I was thankful she didn't ask me to stop associating with her. Back then, it wasn't cool to be seen hanging out with a pregnant girl. Maybe my mom sympathized with her, because she had been a teen mom herself. I don't know, but looking back I think it was really cool of her to let me keep my friendship with

Sidney. Eventually Sidney left my school, and went to another Catholic School, but we always stayed in touch with each other.

In 1976, my sister Andrea was born. She was an 'oopsie' baby, because my parents had no intention of having her. I really loved Andrea and I was very protective of her. I couldn't understand why everyone wanted to hold her. It really irritated me. That's when we all realized that I was possessive and territorial.

In 1980, when Andrea was four years old my second sister was born. During that time, things were getting really bad between my mother and father. Their drug usage had really intensified, and it was causing problems in the family, and their marriage. My mother really wanted to leave my father, but then she got pregnant again. They both really hoped it was a boy thinking that might bring them closer together, and perhaps slow up the whole drug thing. When the baby came and was a girl, it made things worse. My parents had another excuse to continue getting high.

The Home Stretch

These events ushered me into my first two years of high school. Being in the 9th grade confirmed that I was a teenager and I was excited! The Villa Angela Academy had accepted me into their high school program and it was a great honor. The Academy was very selective about who they admitted and I was the first one to be accepted in my family. I was making straight A's and my relatives bragged to all their friends about me. I also excelled at playing the flute, just like my mother. Everyone was happy and sure that things were going great for me, but what they didn't know is that I had started smoking marijuana.

It all began with the three Tracy's. They were my friends in my class, and they all had the same name. I would have to address them by their full name, so they knew which one of them I was talking to. Every day after school, we would all walk to the bus stop together. The Villa Angela Academy sat way back on a lake so we would have to walk up to the street to stand at the bus stop, and it was a long way. That's when the three Tracy's would pull out the weed, and 'pass the joint' back and forth between them. They would also pass it to me, and I would always turn it down. Now, here's the powerful thing about peer pressure. Even though I grew up with parents who were smoking their lives away and I saw the effect it had on them and the family, it didn't stop me from eventually giving in. So, one day when the joint was passed my way, instead of waving it away I surprised them all and took the joint out of Tracy's hand. I held it up to my mouth and took a long, slow hit, inhaling the smoke deep in my lungs. Everyone stopped, and looked at me in amazement! Of course, they were shocked that I actually took a hit off the joint. But, what really freaked them out was that I knew exactly how to hold it, and how to keep the smoke deep in my lungs to get the maximum effect. I pulled on that joint like an old pro and I guess that after years of watching my parents and their friends get high, I probably was. When I exhaled I coughed and choked, barely able to get my breath. There was a long silence then all three Tracy's looked at me with suspicion. The big question was, "When did you learn how to smoke weed like that?" I could have responded by telling them the story about my parents' drug involvement and my years of being exposed to it, but I decided not to. It was much more interesting keeping them in suspense.

After that, getting high with the Tracy's became a regular thing. We had a good time, but it didn't last long. I still had asthma really bad and inhaling the smoke exaggerated my condition. Each time I smoked, I would have trouble breathing and a couple of times I had a mild asthma attack. It just wasn't worth the drama so I eventually stopped smoking, and never went back to it. Now that I think about it, my health issues probably started because I inhaled so much smoke at an early age. It probably caused the asthma that has troubled me for most of my life. I think that's a shame, and probably considered child abuse.

Unlike me, the three Tracy's were doing all the things that most teenagers do, including having sex, and once again they tried to persuade me to do the same. It was as if the devil had placed the Tracy's in my life to lead me down the wrong path, but this time it didn't work. I was afraid of sex and I just didn't want to get into it.

On the weekend, the four of us would hang out at somebody's house and one by one each Tracy would go into a bedroom to have sex. I would sit in the living room by myself and watch TV until they were all done. I remember the look that each of them had as they came out of the bedroom. It was a shameful, sheepish look. They actually looked kind of dirty and I was always glad that I didn't do it.

"How was it?" I would ask each of them. Sometimes the response would be, "It was good!" or sometimes it would be, "Hum, I've had better." I really didn't care how good it was and I only asked, because I didn't know what else to say. It was odd. Even though I wasn't in their clique and I wasn't doing the things that they were doing, they were still really cool with me. Go figure.

After the tenth grade I left Villa Angela. I was tired of going to Catholic Schools and I wanted to experience a public school. I knew that my mother wouldn't agree, mainly because we lived in the inner city. Even then, the stigma was that inner city schools were sub-standard and unsafe and I knew my mother would never give me permission to go. I had to find an alternative. I searched around, and found a college prep school called, The Jane Adams Business Career Center. I attended Jane Adams for my 11th and 12th grades. My mom was mad as all get out that I gave up my place at Villa Angela, because it was such an achievement to be there. What really pissed her off was that I left the school without consulting her.

During that time, I had serious doubts about my parent's ability to make sound decisions for me. They were full blown addicts, and barely able to function. Out of necessity, I started making decisions for myself. I was smart and strong and very determined to have the successful life that my mother and father never had. Leaving Villa Angela and going to The Jane Adams Business Career Center, was the smart thing to do.

I did my research and once I made up my mind, I went to Villa Angela and told them that I was leaving. I then enrolled in the Jane Adams Business Career Center all without my mother's knowledge, or consent. That shows how business minded and determined I was. What really surprised me is that no one thought to consult my parents. I knew that my mother was furious with me, but I didn't care, because Jane Adams was the best place for me to be. It actually proved to be better for me than all the other schools I had attended. It's there that I started my training in accounting and I did very well. I followed in my mother's footsteps. She had completed two years of college for accounting and I pursued accounting. I even joined a prestigious accounting organization. They would send us to different locations to compete with other students that were trained in computerized accounting and I won a lot of trophies.

The whole experience was very stimulating, and encouraging, and I could not have gotten that at Villa Angela.

By the time I reached the 12th grade, I was really excelling in bookkeeping and the school helped me to get a job at a major check-cashing company in Cleveland. I was the bookkeeper's assistant and he taught me everything that I know. He was a very nice man and I stayed at that job for five and a half years. When I look back at all the major decisions that I made by myself, I couldn't help but be proud, because they all turned out well for me.

Chapter Two
"Transition"

"It isn't where you come from; it's where you're going that counts."
Ella Fitzgerald [4]

People say that time is speeded up, and in my case it seems to be true. The years flew by and I couldn't believe that I was actually graduating from high school. I applied to colleges, and was accepted by Baldwin Wallace College, the school of my choice in Berea, Ohio. The three Tracy's, who had followed me from Villa Angela to the Jane Adams Business School followed my lead, and applied to Baldwin Wallace College. In fact, a lot of the Jane Adams students applied to Baldwin College, but I was the only one accepted. I believe that my grades played a large part in that, but I also believe that my involvement in the accounting organization at Jane Adams also played a part.

Unfortunately, when I started college I didn't have the money that I needed for my classes or my living expenses. I had some money saved up for bedding and other stuff for my room, but I needed major financing for my tuition and room and board. I called my grandmother on my mother's side a week before I was supposed to check into my dorm and she came to the rescue. Surprisingly, my mother also snapped out of her drug-induced state just long enough to help me get more money and boy was I was happy! It was all gravy and the job I started while I was still in high school was very accommodating with my school schedule. They kept me on staff and periodically gave me work. It was great, because they had a lot of locations near my school.

I loved the college, and my dorm. It was co-ed, with three floors and the second floor was for boys only. There was one boy named Glenn from New York. He would spend the night with me every night to keep me company. We would sleep in the same bed and play with each other, but we never had full-fledged sex. I was still a virgin. Shortly after that, Glenn left school and I lost track of him.

Once Glenn was gone, I started getting distracted from school. I had always been a good student, but now I couldn't seem to focus at all. I had my parents and their addiction heavy on my mind, and I worried about my two sisters who were still at home. Plus, I was still caught up in being a teenager with everything that entails. There was just a lot going on with me.

Sowing my Wild Oats

I started hanging out with two girls named, Nicole and Angela. They were both party girls that hung out with rappers. I didn't know any rappers so hanging out with them was super exciting to me. I was a sheltered, over-protected girl with a Catholic school upbringing. I had done my little share of partying, but I never experienced it on that level. When Nicole and Angela invited me to a party there would always be celebrities there. We would go to exclusive events, and mingle with rap stars and their entourages. I was in awe of how connected Nicole and Angela were and I felt privileged to be moving in those circles with them.

I was about 18 when Nicole, Angela and I went to a concert in Dayton, Ohio. I didn't know that both of them had boyfriends working crew for the concert. The show was great, but once it was over Nicole and Angela told me to wait while they went behind stage to say goodbye to their boyfriends. They promised me that they would be right back, but an hour later I was still standing around waiting, like a fool. It was a replay of my times with the Tracy's, where I sat around waiting on them while they had sex with their boyfriends. In this case, I was still waiting when everyone was gone and the workers had started cleaning up the concert hall. I couldn't believe it. I was so embarrassed. I looked at the door hoping to see Nicole and Angela and I saw this handsome man, instead. He walked in and came over to where I was standing. I didn't know who he was, but he started talking to me, and told me that his name was Oscar. We started a conversation and I told him about my friends leaving me stranded with no money and no transportation. He was a nice guy and he stayed with me until Nicole and Angela came back. I told him that I was from Cleveland and he said that he would be in Cleveland the following week. He really wanted to get to know me, so we decided to meet up when he came to town. He asked me for my phone number and I gave it to him and as soon as I did, Nicole and Angela walked through the door. Hours had passed and I was furious with them, but I was also glad because if they had not left me I would not have met Oscar.

Everyday I waited for Oscar's call, but it never came. I was starting to get really discouraged until finally one day, he called. He was in Cleveland and wanted to hook up with me. I was so excited! I really liked Oscar. He had won me over when he took away my shame by standing with me in that concert hall in Dayton. I have never forgotten it. I agreed to meet up with him and that started a whole week of fun!

Oscar was only in Cleveland a week, so we tried to

cover all the bases. We went to the movies, the mall, the park, the beach, the club; we went everywhere. We hung out really enjoying each other's company. I started to notice that everywhere we went people would be pointing at him and waving, trying to get his attention. There was such a buzz around him that I finally asked him who he was, and he told me he was the rapper, Black Cole! I was shocked! Here I was, hanging out with a celebrity rapper and I didn't even know it. I had no experience with rappers, accept the ones that Nicole and Angela had introduced me to. It was cool to be with someone that everybody wanted to hang with and I genuinely enjoyed his company. He was so cool and so much fun. I never had that much fun with any of the men I dated. I still remember the movie we went to see called, 'I'm Gonna Get You Sucka'. That movie was hilarious and we laughed so hard and long that I thought that I was going to pass out. I had a great time with Black Cole, and I'll never forget it.

I was still a virgin when I met Black Cole, so we

didn't have sex. We just enjoyed each other's company. Through him, I also met Lil Soul and Lil Soul's promoter, Charles Brown and we are still friends today. I realize now that I was so naïve. I thought that Black Cole and I could have a lasting relationship without having sex. I was wrong. Fortunately, we did stay friends for years and occasionally I would go to California to visit him.

Shortly after, when I was almost nineteen I met my first real boyfriend, Reggie Smith. He was also my first lover and the man that took my virginity. I'll never forget Reggie, because he taught me everything sexually, including oral sex. He was a very good lover as far as I knew, since I had no one else to compare him to.

The first time Reggie and I had sex was crazy. I told him I was a virgin, but he didn't believe me. He was very gentle with me, but not because he thought I was a virgin. I'm sure like most of us, he grew up with people who started having sex at a very young age. He actually started having sex when he was young. That's why he was so experienced. He looked at me as an attractive, outgoing person and he just couldn't believe that I had never had sex. It was so funny, because even though I kept telling him, he didn't believe me and didn't prepare. I tried to warn him, but he just ignored me until he felt the warm blood trickling down my legs and all over his bed! He was shocked, but my attitude was, "I tried to tell you". That whole scene was a dramatic entry into womanhood.

Reggie was a pretty boy and I really liked him. After all, he was my first, but he was also trouble. He needed help financially and I really tried to help him. The kicker is, I didn't know he was using drugs. He actually had a really bad drug addiction. I should have recognized the signs after growing up with parents who did drugs, but I didn't. Maybe being around addicts was so normal for me that I just didn't notice it. Whatever the case, I was really trying hard to help him. As a result, I made some really bad decisions that ruined my credit. But, that wasn't all. Reggie, the man who took my virginity also gave me chlamydia and he acted stupid like he didn't know he had it.

"Reggie! I went to the clinic today and he said, I have chlamydia!"

"Chlamydia? Were did you get that from?" he replied, with a cheap look on his face.

"Where do you think I got it from? You're the only man I'm having sex with, you dirty low down, dog!" I screamed at him.

"Wait a minute, baby. You carrying this too far! Maybe the doctor made a mistake. Maybe it's not chlamydia. Maybe it's some kind of rash or something."

I tell you the truth. If I had a gun in my hand, I would have shot him dead! I know that God was with me, because I only had that one chlamydia outbreak and I never had another one. I didn't even need medication. Thank you Lord! Of course Reggie had to go. I broke up with him the same day, and never looked back.

My next boyfriend was Tony Black who we called Saul. Like every other black male at that time, he thought he was a rapper. He would put together these lame rhymes, and beg me to listen to them.

"Baby, hold up. You got to check these lyrics out. They came to me while I was on the porcelain throne."

'On the toilet, really?' I was thinking. 'Please God, let this one be short.'

"Baby, check it out. *The Man got the plan, making my feet sink in quick sand!* Whoa, baby! What you think?"

"I think you should get a job, that's what I think."

"Oh, there you go, baby. You can't be jealous of your man's success. You got to support him. My career gone buy you diamonds and furs."

"Forget the fur coats and diamond rings. Can you just pay for the toilet paper while you getting your inspiration on the porcelain throne?" I picked up my coat and walked out the door, slamming it as I left.

The miracle is, I stayed with Saul for four years, but we never had sex. After Reggie, I was traumatized sexually and I decided to put sex on the back burner.

Saul and I would talk on the phone sometimes and go out occasionally, but no sex was involved. I eventually got tired of dealing with him and his fake rap career, so I broke up with him, too. It's so tripped out, because his family started accusing me of breaking his heart, and destroying his career. What career? They could not accept that Saul was the problem; he had no talent.

That whole thing really bothered me and I called my friend Sidney to talk about it. Sidney has a way of helping me come out of a funk and gain clarity when things get muddy in my life. Sidney and I don't talk much, but the bond we made as children, still remains. Maybe you have a friend like that. Your lives have changed and you're not around each other that much, but you know that if you need something or if they need something, you're always be there for each other. That's the way it is with Sidney and I. My new friends come and go, but Sidney remains a staple in my life. That's why I called her with the Saul thing and as usual,

Sidney talked me back to reality and I was able to let it go. That's what good friends do.

Through my relationships with Reggie and Saul, I was still kicking it with Nicole and Angela. I don't know why, but out of nowhere they both started accusing me of trying to take everybody's man. Nicole's mother thought I was trying to take her husband and her sister thought I was trying to take her boyfriend. I don't know why, because. I wasn't fast and I didn't dress provocatively. I was actually quiet, and kind of shy. That's how I was raised, and I was still that way. I don't know where it came from, because I definitely wasn't interested in their men. All I can think is that the men were giving the impression that I was coming on to them, when in reality, they were coming on to me.

One day Nicole told me that her boyfriend Keith was coming to town and that he was bringing two friends with him. When the day came, Nicole, Angela and I went to the hotel to see them. It was supposed to be the three of us kicking it with the three of them. When we got there and knocked on his hotel door, Keith looked out, saw it was Nicole, and didn't open the door for us. I was really embarrassed for her, but she kept trying to play it off, saying, "He's just acting silly." But, it was more than that, because he never answered the door and Nicole never saw him during his trip to Cleveland. Nicole thought every man wanted her. She was living in some kind of la-la land, and created the whole relationship with this guy, in her head. The reality was that Keith would talk on the phone with her occasionally, but he never hung out with her. I found out later that he was a drug dealer, and was in Cleveland to negotiate a drug deal, not to kick it with Nicole.

After that, Nicole, Angela and I would go to Delaware so that Nicole could see Keith. She obviously wasn't giving up and if he wouldn't come to Cleveland to see her, she would go to Delaware to see him. During this time, Nicole was also having serious problems with her mother and her mother asked her to move out. I told

Nicole that she could come and stay with me. After moving in, Nicole would spend hours on my phone talking to Keith and occasionally he'd say, "Hi", to me. We would exchange a few words, but that was all the interaction we had. Shortly after moving in with me, Nicole and her mother made up and Nicole moved back home.

One day, Keith called my house. I was surprised, because I figured he knew that his girl didn't live with me anymore. I proceeded to tell him that Nicole had moved and he said he knew and that he called to talk to me. I couldn't believe it. I know that I should have told him off and hung up on him, but I didn't. I don't know why. Maybe I was attracted to him. I don't know, but for weeks we played this cat and mouse game with him trying to persuade me to talk to him. Eventually I gave in. After a while, we started to get really close and I eventually made a trip to Delaware to see him. There were two important things that were memorable about that trip. First, I experienced my first orgasm, which was great. But, here's the kicker. I also got pregnant! I found out two weeks after returning to Cleveland. I called Keith to talk about it and that's when I found out that he already had five children and he wasn't taking care of any of them. I also found out that he treated his past girlfriends really bad, and that he didn't treat his children any better. I knew then that I could not have that man's baby. I told him that I wanted an abortion and that I didn't have the money to get it, so he promised to send me the money. Of course, it never arrived. Then he then told me to come to Delaware to have the abortion, but I found out that he was really trying to trick me. I don't remember how I found out, but I did. I don't know what he was going to do to me, or maybe he was going to try to persuade me to have the baby. I don't know, but I do know that it was a good thing I didn't go.

At that point I knew that I had to have the abortion, but I also knew that I didn't have the money to get it. If only I had insurance. Then I remembered my father had insurance through his job with the City of Cleveland and they paid 100% for abortions. I called the company and they told me my father had let the policy lapse, so I had to pay money to reinstate it. What I also found out was that my father stopped paying the insurance, because he had long since been terminated from his job. The freaky thing is, my father left the house everyday like he was going to work. He never told anybody that he was fired. I couldn't believe it! The news hit me like a punch to the stomach. My father was in much worse shape than I thought.

Fortunately for me, Kaiser allowed me to reinstate the policy and boy was I grateful. Having insurance cost a whole lot less than trying to pay for the abortion myself! There was one thing I didn't understand. When I reinstated the insurance I was only two weeks pregnant, but because of some weird clause in the policy, I had to wait until I was two months pregnant to have the abortion. Maybe for some women that was a good thing; it gave them time to think about, and perhaps change their mind about the abortion. For me, it wasn't. There was no way I was having Keith's baby.

Finally, the abortion was done. The doctor told me not to have sex for six weeks, and to follow up with a physician. I chose Planned Parenthood. I will never forget how kind and helpful they were to me at a time when I needed it most. They were very in tune with my needs as a woman. For that reason, I'm an advocate for Planned Parenthood and I've been a patient with them ever since. After that whole ordeal, I never saw Keith again. "Good riddance."

One thing I have to say is that during that time, I never had a shortage of men. I attracted them like flies to honey and as soon as I ended one relationship, another one began. After Keith, I met Jason. Everyone knew him and he seemed nice, like someone I could really get into. He was a tall guy, 6'4", with a pretty brown complexion. Jason was actually really nice looking and we dated for two years.

After about a year, I didn't like what I was seeing. All Jason did from morning to night was sit around and get high. Here was this lazy, weed smoking, not knowing what to do with his life kind of guy, and I didn't like it. I was a hustler and I was always working in accounting. Even though they were entry-level jobs, I was bringing in more than my share of money.

After talking to Jason, he said he was going to change and I gave him the benefit of the doubt, staying with him another year. Once the year passed, not only had Jason not changed, he was worse. We would have long heated arguments about it and every time Jason would promise to get up off his butt and do something. But, he never did. I had to be real with myself. I could never be happy with a man who did nothing but get high, so I broke up with Jason. It hurt us both to split up, because we were really feeling each other. Unfortunately, our ideas were really different about what a man's role should be in a relationship, so for my own sanity I moved on.

When I look back, I realize that I've always had a pattern of hooking up with men that were no good for me. They were either heavily into using or selling drugs, or were whores, lazy, or had no respect or appreciation for women. I was real smart when it came to business and accounting, but in romance I was so naive. I believe it's because I grew, as one of my boyfriends called me, "a lame", with a Catholic school upbringing. I had never lived a hard, fast life.

I was a virgin longer than anyone that I knew, so I had no real experience with men. I honestly believe that the men I dated knew that I was inexperienced and took advantage of me. The older I get, the more I realize that I'm not alone in this. There are many women who put their love and trust in men who are just not worth it, and the reasons are different for each woman. Some have grown up without a loving father figure, and don't know how to receive love from a man. Members of their own family, like a father or brother or even a female relative, abused many women. In many cases, these women become angry and bitter, and take it out on their significant others. They basically become abusers themselves. Women like me were sheltered, and didn't have the opportunity to interact with boys on a regular basis. Being in Catholic schools most of my childhood, and having a very strong family unit, I was kept away from boys. I had no experience and when I started dating and I was way too trusting and so naïve.

I had a close relationship with my father who loved me, but he was totally dysfunctional. So, I attracted dysfunctional men, and fell into traps that could have been avoided. It's sort of a catch 22. If you hang out in the streets at a young age, you get bruised and abused, and grow up wise, but cynical and untrusting. But, if you stay sheltered, and grow up without experience, you fall prey to wolves looking for innocent sheep to devour. It seems like a no win situation. That's where God comes in.

I've learned through the pain of my relationships, that you have to seek guidance and direction from God in all your relationships. Only He has the power to heal, guide, and protect us from the pitfalls of life. Even if we do get hurt, God can heal us and make us whole again, so that we can get up and start anew. In my case, it took me many years to learn this simple truth and as a result, I've suffered many years of pain and abuse.

At this point, I'm in my second year of college and I had to drop out. I was out of funds and I couldn't get help anywhere for the kind of money I needed. I decided to move in with my parents so I could work and save up the money to go back to school. That plan turned out to be a disaster, because by then, both my parents were full-fledged crack addicts. I just couldn't deal with it. Everyday I watched both of them waste away and there was nothing I could do about it. I was in hell and my sadness was almost unbearable. I suffered even more than my sisters. When they came along, my parents were already moving toward addiction so their behavior was normal for my sisters, but not for me. I remember when my parents were young and vibrant, and full of hope and anticipation for the future. I saw their speedy progression from alcohol to hash, and on to harder drugs. I witnessed their decline from functioning members of society, to mere perversions of their former selves. With all my heart I hated to see them like that, but I knew that there was nothing I could do about it. I still remembered my dad cooking up Hash in the kitchen when I was three. That was many years past. Since then it had all escalated. My parents had graduated from the fun and seeming innocence of drinking and smoking hash, to the tragedy of being addicted to crack cocaine! My father took it even further, and became addicted to heroin, too. I knew in my heart, that only God could deliver them from those demons.

I had recently met a new friend named Tawana Thomas and I talked to her a lot about my parents' addiction. I was so depressed and I would share those dark feelings with her. The funny thing is, Tawana always responded with the same idea, "The only way to beat depression is to go out and meet some guys!" I didn't know what else to do, so I took her advice. I shook off the depression and got back in the dating game. I had broken up with Jason six months prior, so I was definitely game to meet a new man. That's when

Tawana told me about her friend, Roberto Montana.

Chapter Three
"The Counterfeit"

"True glory takes root, and even spreads; all false pretences, like flowers fall to the ground; nor can any counterfeit last long."
Marcus Tillius Cicero [5]

Tawana set me up with her friend, Roberto, and we ended up double dating with Tawana and her boyfriend. Roberto really impressed me. He was handsome and seemed really nice. He was also from the Dominican Republic, and that was a first for me. That night we all got together and went to a great restaurant called, Shooters. We had a good time, drinking Champagne all night. I'll never forget how surprised I was, when I couldn't decide between two entrees, and Roberto told me to order both. None of my previous boyfriends would have offered that. Rob treated me really well and I was glad to be out with him. After dinner, he took me home and kissed me before he left, and I couldn't wait to call Tawana to talk about Mr. Roberto Montana.

A few days later, Roberto picked me up and took me to his house. It was a really nice place right on the waterfront in Euclid. When we got there, I was really surprised, because the place was empty. He had no furniture, so I turned him right back around and took him shopping to decorate his apartment. We went to store after store, buying furniture, bedding, a TV, food, and a lot more stuff. Once we put everything in place, his apartment finally looked like a home, and Roberto was grateful for my help. After that, he really rolled out the red carpet for me, and to show his gratitude, he finished the day off by giving me a long, sensual, bath.

I had been in the tub with a man before, but I had never experienced a bath like the one Roberto gave me. First, he didn't get in the tub with me. Rob made me vulnerable, as he sat on the side of the tub, fully dressed. His eyes poured over my body, and I could feel the goose bumps form on my arms. My face flushed a bright red, as Roberto took his time, drinking in every curve of my body. When he took the soft cloth and touched the hollow of my neck, my body twitched, as I breathed in deeply. Rob used the soft cloth to make slow, small circles on my flesh, pausing to tenderly dab each one of my nipples. Each one of them swelled, engorged with blood. He slowly slid the cloth down my stomach, to my pubic hairs, swirling the cloth in my hairs. I couldn't take it anymore. I arched my crouch up to meet his hand, but he only rubbed the hairs and the fat swollen lips that folded over my clitoris. I started to moan and thrash around in the water. I wanted him to rub my clit. It was aching for it. Rob lightly ran the cloth over my clit once, then twice. If he had touched it one more time, I would have exploded in the warm sudsy water. Rob knew better than that. He wanted to make it slow and excruciating. He let the cloth float in the tub, and picked up the bar of lightly scented soap. Rob rubbed it all over each of my breasts. Then, he took his fingers and ever so lightly circled each nipple with the soap subs. I gasped in heat, longing for his lips to suckle my breasts. As if he could read my thoughts, Rob took a handful of water and poured it over my breasts, staring at me, as he eased down to his knees. I was surprised as he roughly grabbed both breasts and pushed them together, allowing the fat, straining nipples to touch. He leaned in and put both nipples in his mouth, suckling them like a baby. I moaned loud, as he sucked harder and harder, until I could feel my love juices gush into the water. Rob abruptly stopped and leaned over to whisper in my ear, "You wanna cum"? I breathed in a deep breath and hoarsely replied, "Yeah", I moaned back. To finish me off, Rob took one of my legs and laid it over the side of the tub and laid the over leg over the other side. With my pussy gapped open for him to see, he took his fingers and rubbed my clit fast and hard, as his other hand pinched each of my nipples. It only took a minute for me to arch my pelvis up and scream out one of the hardest climaxes I had ever experienced. The whole time, Rob was looking me in the eyes, drinking in the lust he created in me. I slid down in the tub, spent, and Roberto had me stand, as he washed the soap off of me and wrapped me in a warm, fuzzy robe. That day with Roberto was clearly the best date I had ever had, and he was the first man that had treated me so good. I was really starting to fall for him.

Things were going good with Rob, until something started happening that wasn't normal. I would be hanging out in Rob's apartment and kicking it with him for days. Then suddenly, he would usher me out to take me back home, and I wouldn't see him again for a long time. Then suddenly, with no prior notice, he would show up and take me home with him. We would pick up where we left off, as if he had never left. It was strange, and it really baffled me. I never heard of anyone doing that, and my question was, "Where did he go when he left, and why did he go for so long?" The answer came one day when I was talking to a friend about it. She looked at me as if to say, "You mean you don't know?" I still didn't understand until she blurted out,

"You got to know Roberto is selling drugs, right?"

"Selling drugs?" I replied in disbelief.

"Yeah, in a big way, and I heard his brother is slingin' too. He some kind of boss."

Whoa! My head was spinning. Now, it all made sense. Here I was thinking he had another woman, when he was really leaving me to take care of drug business. It kind of shook me, but I have to admit, it excited me, too. I was dating a Dominican drug kingpin. Well, hot damn!

After processing the whole thing, I realized that dating a man with Rob's kind of money was a good thing, even if it was drug money. Roberto was my ticket out of my parent's house. I was raw from the pain of their addictions, and it was too much for me. I told Rob what was going on, and that I needed his help to move out. I'm sure he knew my parents were addicts, and he was more than willing to help me. One day, right after our conversation, Rob came to my house and left a navy blue leather coach, love seat and chair in the hallway. We lived in a two family home and Roberto left the furniture in the hallway for a long time. My family were so irritated.

Finally, one day Roberto showed up on my doorstep. I was so glad. He surprised me because he had found me a really nice apartment about 10 minutes from my parent's house. It had high-end finishes, and the most beautiful hardwood floors I had ever seen. Rob paid the $300 deposit, and moved me in. My parents took it really hard when I left, especially my mother. She was devastated. She had missed me when I went to college, and now I was leaving again. Sometimes I think I was a bright light in her otherwise dark, world. I didn't know that for sure, but what I did know was that I had to move. I couldn't take the darkness anymore, and I was happy when my moving day finally came. As soon as Roberto paid for everything and got me settled into the apartment, he left again. Fortunately, I was able to maintain the apartment with my accounting and temp jobs.

The night that I moved in, Rob took me out on a double date with two of his friends. The man was the same guy that Tawana had brought on our double date, when I first met Rob. It was odd, because I thought he was Tawana's boyfriend. If they weren't dating, they sure acted like it. The new girl's name was Allison Brooks. Now, I'm a very nurturing person, and I'll listen to anyone with a problem. That night, Allison told me she was really down on her luck, and was about to be homeless. She also said she had a daughter, who was staying with her aunt. If I were thinking, I would have asked her why she couldn't stay with her aunt also. Instead I said, "Why don't you stay with me until you find your own place? I've got two bedrooms and there's plenty of room." She was ecstatic and accepted my offer without any hesitation.

After Allison moved in and we got settled and comfortable with each other, we had a big housewarming party. My cousin Callie and all of our friends came. It was a great party, and everyone had a really good time. At some point, the phone rang. I answered and when I realized it was Jason, I handed the phone to someone else and they passed it to someone, who passed it to someone, until it finally landed in the hands of someone who was sober enough to talk to him. Apparently, he wanted to know my new address, and the person, who I didn't even know, gave it to him. I was mad, but I didn't make a big deal out of it. Jason was out of my life and I had no intention of bringing him back in.

Rob spent the night and the next morning, he left to go to the store. Shortly after, there was a knock on the door. I immediately opened it thinking Rob must have forgotten his wallet or something, and there stood Jason. He apparently had been sitting outside in a car, waiting for Rob to leave to make his move. I was startled, as he pulled out a gun and pointed it in my face. I starting screaming, and ran into the house, with Jason chasing after me. I was terrified when he grabbed me, and leaned real close into my face. He put the gun to my head and whispered in my ear, "Six months is too soon to find another boyfriend." Then after scaring me half to death, he put the gun away and left just as fast as he came. I stood frozen, in total shock. What in the world was that?

When I look back on it, Jason never intended to hurt me. If he did, he could easily have shot me. What he wanted was to scare me, because his ego was so bruised. He wanted me to feel the pain he felt and he totally succeeded! After that, I didn't hear from Jason for years and I decided not to tell Roberto about it. I didn't want to start a war. Considering the kind of people that they both were, I knew someone would have gotten killed.

Months passed and Allison never found her own place. The timing was really bad because my temp work wasn't coming in, and I definitely couldn't pay all the rent myself. Roberto had, once again, dropped off the face of the earth, so he wasn't around to help me. Allison and I just couldn't keep up, and we eventually got evicted.

Fortunately for me, I found another place just in time, and I moved in with Tawana Thomas, the friend that had introduced me to Rob. The place was on Martin Luther King Boulevard and Union. Martin Luther King was a long, wide street and the neighborhood was nice. Our apartment was on the first floor of a two family home. From the outside, it looked like one big, really nice house.

Crossing the Line

To make sure we had the money to pay the rent, Tawana and I started stealing from department stores. We would go to high-end stores, and steal, really nice clothes. We were both fashion conscious and wanted to look good, but we didn't have the money to buy anything, so we stole them. We would sport the clothes we liked, and sell the rest. This went on for a while. We even brought in my cousin, and some of our friends, and taught them how to steal. The crazy thing is, I had no experience with stealing. Growing up, I wasn't around thieves, and as far as I knew, no one in my family ever stole anything. So, why I thought I could choose that lifestyle and get away with it really baffles me. The truth is, I had no experience, and was no good at taking what didn't belong to me. I was on a fast moving train, headed for a crash.

Between us all, I was the worse. I would walk in the store looking so suspicious. Sometimes a clerk would look at me like I was some kind of strange bird. I guess I was shaking and looking really weird, but whatever the case, my day came and I found myself sitting in the security office of one of the most expensive stores in the nation, charged with theft.

Now, its one thing to play the role of criminal, and it's quit another one, to be treated like one. I was clearly in some kind of fantasy world, where you could do what you wanted and never suffer the consequences. Well, being led to that security office snatched me out of that fantasy world, into the real world, and it was cold and terrifying. That's the thing about embracing the darkness. You can never walk away, unscathed. In my case, I was facing jail time, and the reality of that felt like a cold glass of ice water was thrown in my face.

Fortunately for me, my friend, Attorney Wilson, agreed to represent me. He knew all the judges and lawyers in the city, and he would always miraculously work it out for me. I said always, because I wasn't just charged once. No! As soon as I got off on the first charge, I went back into the stores and started stealing again. Now, considering how bad a thief I was, it wasn't long before I got caught again, and again, and each time Wilson was able to work something out for me. The last time Wilson represented me, he turned and looked at me and said, "Cynthia, please stop it! Can't you see you're not good at it?" I looked in his eyes and for the first time, I realized he was right. I was a horrible thief, and that was the last time that I stole anything. Surprisingly, Tawana stopped stealing too, and we managed to keep our bills paid without it. The truth always dispels the darkness, and I thanked God, that phase of my life was over!

You know, when I look back, I realize I had a lot to be grateful for. Any one of the things that had happened to me, the bad relationships, the gun in my face, the stealing, could have ruined my life forever. I now know that if it weren't for God, I wouldn't be sharing my story with you. As we're living the crazy experiences that we all have, we don't realize how close to the edge of destruction we are. Only the grace and mercy of a loving God can carry us through those seasons, a little bruised, but still standing.

This time when Roberto left, he was gone longer than ever, and I was really concerned. I tried to figure out where he could be, but I just didn't know. One night I got dressed and went to the club to have some fun, and to take my attention off of Rob. At one point, I went to the bathroom, and while I was in the stall, I overheard some girls talking about Roberto and his girlfriend. I couldn't believe it! I mean, what is the chance that I just happened to be in a bathroom at a club, trying to get Roberto off my mind, and some random girls start talking about Rob. It just didn't make any sense. I wanted to hear more clearly, so I came out of the stall and pretended to be combing my hair and fixing my makeup in the mirror, while I listened. I found out that not only did Roberto have a girlfriend, but they also had a child. I could not believe it. I was so upset! I left the club and called my best friend Sidney, to tell her all about it.

Thankfully, a few days later Roberto showed up, and I really let him have it. "Why couldn't you be honest with me?" I yelled at him! "Why did you have to play this game with me?" I cried and yelled, and yelled and cried! I couldn't understand why he was trying to pull the wool over my eyes. It was bad enough that I couldn't depend on him. He was in and out of my life like a revolving door, with no notice and no explanation, and now this. It was way too much and just like I did with the other guys that didn't live up to the standards that any decent woman would expect from a man, I let Roberto go. I made the decision not to see him again, and I moved on with my life.

It wasn't hard to let go of Rob. Maybe because he was always leaving me anyway, so I was used to being without him. I was shocked when six weeks later, Donald English, a childhood friend that I had known since the fifth grade, came to my apartment. He pulled out a newspaper and showed me a story written about Roberto and some of his business associates. The article said that Roberto Montana was in jail as part of a big drug conspiracy in Cleveland. I couldn't believe it. This was really, really serious, and even though I knew that Roberto was dealing drugs, I still felt really bad for him. Yes, he lied to me, and yes he led me on, knowing that he had a girlfriend and a child. In spite of all that, I couldn't forget that Roberto had done a lot of good things for me. He helped me get an apartment, he bought me furniture, well maybe he didn't buy it, but still, he gave it to me. Rob would give me money, and show me a really good time, and I couldn't ignore all that. Besides, I was never one to hold a grudge. Like my mother, I've always had a heart for people, and their sufferings. So, after weighing everything, I was compelled to write Roberto a letter. He responded immediately, and we became friends again. I figured that in his condition, he could really use one.

On the flip side, Tawana and I were doing fine in our place on Martin Luther King and Union. We both paid our part of the rent and split the other bills. Tawana had a friend that we called Jamaican Jackie. Tawana, Jackie and I would go out to the Reggae clubs to party. I really didn't get with the whole reggae, Jamaican thing, but I would go just go to be hanging out. One night at the club I saw Allison, and once again, she was in trouble financially. Allison was always down on her luck. She started sharing with me how bad things were for her and that she had no place to live. My heart was soft and I couldn't help myself, so I invited Allison to come live with me in my room. Tawana and I had a two-bedroom apartment, so, the only place Allison could move into was my room. That night I told Tawana that Allison was moving into my room and she blew up! She absolutely did not want to live with Allison. I guess she had a right to be mad, because I should have consulted her before making that decision. After all, it was Tawana's apartment too. Unfortunately, Tawana couldn't get past it, so shortly after Allison moved in, Tawana moved out. Allison was happy because now she had Tawana's room to herself. Tawana had been a very good roommate, but at this point, it didn't matter. What was done was done.

For a while, things were pretty good for Allison and I. Shortly after Allison moved in, we came up with the idea of having parties at our apartment. As I said before, Martin Luther Boulevard was a large, wide Boulevard that was a very popular street in the city. Everybody came to our street to hang out, and it was wild. All the drug dealers would block up the street with their big fancy cars with all kinds of illegal activity, from drug dealing, sex trading, the selling of hot merchandise, and any other illegal thing you can think of. It was a trip, but we didn't care. We loved it, because it was exciting and we were in party mode. The street we lived on was famous for it. Allison and I decided to get in on the action, so every Tuesday evening we would invite people to our apartment to party. The girl that lived in the apartment above us hated us. She was a single mom with two kids, and we believed that she hated on us, because she couldn't be part of the fun. We could have cared less, because we were having a ball, and didn't have a care in the world. We would invite our friends over to party inside our apartment then move the party outside on the steps. Everybody would see us and come over to party with us. Things got so big, that we moved our parties to the Togo Suite. It was a really nice place that was big enough to hold the crowds. Allison and I were partying on a Tuesday like it was the weekend, and we didn't care what anybody thought about it. Those were the best times we had in that apartment, but unfortunately, the good times.

A Ram in the Bush

All this time, Roberto was still in jail waiting for his trial date. When it finally came, he pleaded, "Not guilty". Everybody knew that Rob was involved in a lot of illegal stuff but he claimed that in this case he wasn't involved, so he fought it. The trial lasted about three weeks. It was 1992 and that's when I met Rob's Attorneys, John Wilson, Jeff Washington, and John Young. They were representing Rob and the other people being charged in the case. As a friend of Rob's, I met with them for lunch to talk about the case. Attorney Young really liked me and he asked for my phone number. I wasn't interested but Attorney Wilson who was in his 60s, also asked me for my number and I gave it to him. It was really funny because Attorney Young wanted to fight Wilson over me. He was young and had a lot of money and he couldn't understand why I preferred the 60 year-old Wilson. I think it was a major blow to his ego, but it was childish and it told me a lot about his character.

Even though I was only 22 years young and John Wilson was in his 60's, I really enjoyed being with him. We actually dated for about a year, and I loved every minute of it. He was a great conversationalist, very smart and I loved listening and learning from him. He took me to lot of fabulous places, including the racetrack where he taught me how to bet on the races. I spent a lot of time with him, even at his office. Wilson wined and dined me and always gave me money. Life was good and I felt really privileged to be dating him.

All my friends were jealous of my relationship with Wilson. They could tell that he really liked me. He would pull up in his shiny, new Cadillac, and pick me up. Then he'd take me to fabulous places and buy me really nice, expensive things. I would come home and tell Allison about the great times we had, and show her the nice things Wilson bought me. My friends had no one in their lives that treated them even half as good.

Their male associates, and they had a lot of them, would have sex with them and that was it. Their men wouldn't ask them if they needed anything, bring them any presents, or do anything for them. Wilson was just the opposite. He made sure I had money for my bills and everything else I needed. While all of this was going on, I found out from Attorney Young that Wilson was married. I figured he was, but it didn't matter to me. Wilson was good to me and whenever he wasn't in court, he was with me. At 22 years old that was good enough for me.

During that time Jason came back in the picture. I saw him out at a club one night and we reconnected, but only as casual friends. The freaky thing is that Jason had a friend who worked as a receptionist in Wilson's law firm. One day Jason called me and said, "So, you're going out of town with that old man, huh? I'm surprised you haven't left yet." I was like, "What are you talking about? I'm not going out of town with Wilson." And I wasn't. Apparently, the receptionist told

Jason that Wilson was out of town with another woman and Jason couldn't wait to tell me. "You mean to tell me old man Wilson is cheating on you, and his wife? That Wilson is a bad dude!" Ragging me on and on.

When Wilson got back, I told him everything his receptionist told Jason and he had a fit! He told the other attorneys in the office and they too were livid! They couldn't believe that she was sharing their personal business. How could they continue to have someone like her working in the firm? What if she shared confidential client information? They could be sued for millions! After weighing everything they really let her have it, then they fired her. When they told her she was fired, she cried her heart out and really made a scene, but it didn't change anything. They threw her out of the office with no remorse. After that incident, I really started dating Wilson in earnest. I couldn't help myself. I really liked him and I guess I was a little jealous of his wife. The cool thing is, Wilson and I are still friends today.

I really needed a car. Because of his driving record, and heavy drinking, Jason knew he shouldn't be driving, so he gave his car to me. It was a beat up old black Grand Prix, but that car was the only good thing that Jason had ever done for me.

Allison stopped paying her rent and I couldn't handle the whole thing by myself. Even though I was still dealing with Wilson, he couldn't pay all of my rent. He had already spent a lot of money on me and had helped pay my part of the rent. To ask him to pay Allison's half too, was just too much so I gave up the apartment and moved in with my grandmother, great grandmother and grandfather. I had my own room, but I was miserable!

At 23 years old, I had finally gotten out on my own, but because of Allison I had to go back home to live with my family. I was really mad about the whole thing, so I called my best friend Sidney. Through it all she had remained my friend and closest confidant. I told her I didn't want to give up and that I wanted to go looking for another apartment. She agreed to go with me, so we drove around looking for another apartment. Everyday we looked and finally I found a place that I could maintain by myself. The rent was only $300 a month and it was nice. I wanted that apartment so bad, that I practically begged the landlord to let me rent the place, so she gave me a chance. I was so grateful and I paid my rent on time every month

To help supplement my income, I started doing manicures and hand massages for men. I had never been trained to be a masseuse, but I instinctively knew how to do it. I saw it as another challenge, so I told everyone I knew that I was in business. I had a lot of clients who used their hands a lot and had problems with stiffness, such as barbers and chefs. I even had my Attorney friend Jeff Washington, as a client. I charged $20 for each service and I made really good money to supplement my income.

In 1993, I met an Attorney named Eduardo White who hooked me up with a job at a law firm. They needed a legal secretary and I pretended that I was a good typist to get the job. The reality was, I couldn't type at all! I was a fast pecker, but I couldn't type without looking at the keyboard. It was crazy, because a legal secretary does a lot of typing. I was really daring back then. At any time, I could have been found out and of course, fired. Because I loved the challenge, I faked it and with all diligence I used a typing tutorial to teach myself how to type. I was on edge everyday, but they never found out my secret and over time I actually became a fast, very good typist.

The firm had eleven black male attorneys, working full-time and they all loved me. Each one of them at some point, would call me into their office to spend time with me, but what they were really doing was looking down my blouse. It took me a while to figure out what they were doing and when I did, I thought it was so funny. Eduardo, the man that hooked me up with the job wanted to date me, but I just didn't like him like that. Plus, it was no surprise that none of the women in the office liked me. I knew they were jealous and I was ok with that. I had plenty of male friends to spend time with.

Shortly after I started working there I met another attorney on staff named, Stan Howard. I heard one of the senior Attorneys call him Stan, so when I would pass him in the hall, I'd say, "Hi, Stan" and he would always smile at me. When other people in the office started hearing me call him Stan, they would get so mad! I think they were jealous, because they didn't have the permission to call any of the attorneys by their first name. They had to call him, "Mr. Howard".

It was a shock to me to find out that years after I left the firm Stan committed suicide. I couldn't believe it. He was apparently very depressed, but he never told anyone. That really hurt me when I found out about it. I wish he had shared his pain with someone or sought professional help. There's a saying that, "We're only as sick as our secrets." That means that when we hide our feelings and issues and refuse to share them with others, they fester inside of us and make us mentally and/or physically ill. We feel trapped in our pain, and believe that there's no way out, then sometimes suicide becomes an option. I believe that if we can look away from our own problems and realize that everyone is dealing with something, we'll recognize that we're not alone. For anyone that has problems, there's always someone worse off. We're all in this thing together and suicide should never be an option.

At the office, one of the other attorneys would call me in to look down my blouse. I didn't mind, because he helped me make money by giving me a lot of extra data entry work. The owner of the firm would also look down my blouse and the other owner who was a jerk, is now a judge. It figures, because he was always very stern and a stickler for everything being exactly by the book.

Tony Lewis, another attorney friend of mine walked in my office one day. When I looked up and saw him I said, "What are you doing here? I'm not doing any work for you!" I met Tony in 1986 and he was the first Attorney that I had ever befriended. I met him after I graduated from Jane Adams. We met at a party and exchanged numbers and talked on the phone a couple of times, then he left to go back to school. He went to Morehouse and then Howard where he met Jeff Washington who recruited him to work at our firm. We rekindled our friendship, and started a coffee club at work. A bunch of us would sit downstairs in the lobby and drink coffee and talk about Seinfeld. It's funny, because at that time I didn't watch Seinfeld. I would laugh and talk and play if off, but I really had no knowledge of what was happening on the Seinfeld show. It was years after our coffee club that I actually started watching Seinfeld.

I was barely getting by financially working at the firm. Even though Tony was there and I had finally started making friends at work, I was really depressed. I didn't think my life was going anywhere and I was stuck in a very negative mindset. I would go home and sit around brooding, and feeling like there was no hope. To top it all off, one morning I went outside and my Grand

Prix wasn't where I left it. At first, I thought that perhaps I had parked it somewhere else, but I soon realized that my car had gotten stolen from in front of my apartment building. It was easy to steal, because the locks on the doors weren't working, so I could never lock it. That didn't help my mood.

Shortly after that, I turned 23 and that birthday started out really bad. I had no plans, so I was just sitting in my apartment feeling sorry for myself. To my surprise, Donald English and Danny Jones came by and told me to get dressed, because they were taking me out for my birthday. I was so shocked, because I didn't expect anyone to remember or to care that it was my birthday and it turned out to be a great day. We went out and I picked out a cake that I really liked. They also bought me some food, and rode me around the city all day to cheer me up. It worked and at least for that day I felt good.

Once my birthday passed, I went right back to being depressed. I had a lot on mind and it was all starting to really bring me down. I was really depressed about my parent's drug addiction and I was having a hard time dealing with Roberto being in prison. I also really thought that after all my studies and accomplishments I would be further along financially. But, I wasn't. I was barely getting by. I didn't have a boyfriend and all the ones in my past all turned out to be no good, even Rob. Even though he did a lot of good things for me, he turned out to be a liar and he never really committed to me. So, on top of everything else I was also lonely and in need of companionship. I would go out to the clubs looking for fun, but I knew that I was wasting my time. My life, as far as I was concerned, was in a shambles.

Chapter Four
"Love Personified"
"When you love a man, he becomes more than a body. His physical limbs expand, and his outline recedes, vanishes. He is rich and sweet and right. He is part of the world, the atmosphere, the blue sky and the blue water." Gwendolyn Brooks [6]

I was lonely and in a constant state of depression. I was still in contact with Roberto, but his trial dragged on and on; it was taking forever! I waited in agony, until the call finally came. The trial was over. I was excited and a little nervous, because no one could predict what the outcome would be.

As I sat in the courtroom as close to Roberto as I could, I could feel my palms sweating. Whatever the judge decided would determine Rob's fate, but it would also determine mine. He was everything to me and I couldn't imagine living without him. Rob loved me, protected me, and took care of all my needs. Without him I would be back to square one, not knowing what to do. It was a sad state of affairs, but I was still hoping for the best.

The bailiff took the paper with the juror's decision to the judge. He looked at it and asked the jury to announce the decision. The lead guy stood up and said, "We the jury find Roberto Montana, guilty of drug trafficking". My stomach felt sick as I saw Rob drop his head in shock. Then the judge told Rob to rise. He slowly stood up, straightened his shoulders and looked the judge dead in the eyes. Even though he knew it was all over, Roberto held his composure and stood up straight like a man.

"Roberto Montana, for the charge of drug trafficking, this court hereby sentences you to thirty-one years and eight months in federal prison!" My heart jumped out of my chest as the judge banged his gavel on the desk!

Thirty-one years and eight months? Roberto would be an old man when he got out! My throat felt like it had a huge boulder on it and I could barely breathe. Roberto had always maintained that he was innocent of the charges that put him in jail, but the truth is, he still had his hands in a lot of illegal activity. I guess it's true what they say, karma is a trip and we all have to pay. In Rob's case, he paid dearly.

Roberto would always call me collect to talk. He was in a horrible situation and needed a lifeline, someone to help him stay sane. I made the decision to be there for him. Roberto had family in the states, but they were all scattered so I was sure no one knew what had happened to Rob. I was the only one he had. Rob's life as he knew it was over and in order to survive he needed a link to his past. I became that link and he focused on me, to keep his attention away from the hell he was living. I think we all at some point in our lives are called to be that anchor, that point of love to help someone survive the storms of life. Little did I know, I would soon be experiencing a series of storms myself and God would send people to offer me a lifeline, just like I had offered to Roberto. It's true that we reap what we sow, good or bad.

My phone bills went through the roof and my phone was always being turned off. There was no way I could keep paying the high phone bills. They made my bleak financial situation, even worse. As time passed, I started going to the jail to see Roberto. I knew a correctional officer inside and he would help me do things that were normally not allowed. I would cook up some good home cooked meals, and give them to the guard for Rob. So, he was eating really well. Even though Roberto had betrayed me by lying about having a girlfriend and a child, I couldn't change the kind of person that I am. My spirit led me to continue to help him.

One day I got a call from a friend of Rob's. He said that he and Roberto had been writing letters to each other. Apparently, Rob's brother Hermes Montana was coming to town, and he wanted to talk to Rob. He asked me if I could help Rob's brother find out how to communicate with him. I told him I'd get back to him. Honestly, I didn't know what I was dealing with and I didn't want to agree to anything without talking to Rob. When I got in touch with him and told him about the phone call, he was ecstatic! Hermes was his half brother. They had the same mother, but different daddies. It didn't matter, because apparently Roberto really loved his brother. He even asked me if Hermes could stay with me while he was in town. I didn't know about that. I didn't know Hermes, and I really wasn't in a relationship with Rob. It just seemed kind of weird to me. Rob kept trying to persuade me by telling me that his brother would pay all of my bills, while he was staying with me. I'm not gone lie. That definitely peeked my interest, because I was having a really rough time financially. It sounded like a good deal, so I agreed.

Hermes was also coming to see his son who lived near me. Apparently he and his son's mother had broken up years ago, on really bad terms. She was bitter and angry, and didn't want him to see his son. It all seemed really messy and I didn't know how it was all going to turn out. I reluctantly waited for the day when Hermes would come.

From Before to After

The day finally came and Hermes arrived at my apartment. This man walked in with an unmistakable air of authority. He was so charismatic, that he scared me. I thought, "Who is this guy?" He looked liked he was the head of some huge cartel and his powerful spirit filled my entire apartment! I tried to hide it, because Hermes was Rob's brother but the truth is, I was irresistibly attracted to him. He was a very handsome Dominican, with dark curly hair, and rich, deep mocha eyes. I found out later that he had just gotten out of federal prison after serving five and a half years. I was really reluctant to open my home to him. I could tell he was into some really deep stuff and I didn't want to be caught up in it.

Hermes quickly scanned my apartment, and then fixed his eyes on me. I felt really uncomfortable. It was an awkward moment and to break the silence, I asked if he wanted to talk to Rob? That lightened Hermes up and he sat his bags down. I called Rob and gave the phone to

Hermes, then I went to the bathroom. I looked at myself in the mirror and I was horrified. My face was pale as a ghost. "Oh, God! Did he notice how he affected me?" I dashed some water on my face, and went back to the living room. Hermes was finishing the call and asked if I wanted to talk to Rob? Maybe he could feel my reluctance to let him stay with me, because when I took the phone Rob practically begged me to let Hermes stay. I didn't want to, but I was kind of curious about him so, I decided to let him stay.

Hermes was very protective of me. Whenever I left the house going to the mall, to the store or wherever, Hermes would say, "Cynthia, where you going?" Then, the second question would be, "Do you need any money?" He was all up in my business. Roberto used to be the same way. I figured it was a Dominican thing, so I let it go.

One day, I invited my girlfriend Myra to the house. Hermes asked me later who she was and that he liked her and wanted to meet her. So, I talked to Myra and told her all about him and she agreed to meet him. We all went to a club that night so they could connect. I was hoping it would turn out to be a hook up between the two of them. That way, maybe he would go stay with her.

When Myra arrived, I made the introductions and after some small talk we went to the club. The objective was for them to spend some time getting to know each other. That was the plan, but it certainly didn't turn out that way. I would walk away from Hermes and Myra, and mingle with other people. I wanted to give them some privacy, but wherever I went Hermes would end up standing right next to me. He was being so protective of me, and honestly I didn't know what to think. I figured that he was doing that Dominican thing again, trying to protect his brother's interest. Whatever it was, it made me very uncomfortable. Hermes was supposed to be spending time with Myra not leaving her sitting alone at the table. I was confused and I felt bad for her. We both went to the bathroom and I asked her what she thought of Hermes? She immediately said, "Cynthia, Hermes doesn't want me. It's you that he wants." I tried to play it off by saying that he was only trying to protect me because of Rob, but truthfully, I knew that he liked me and I had to admit, I really liked him too.

After leaving the club, Hermes and I took Myra home and we headed back to my apartment. It was really quiet in the car, because we both knew that something was brewing between us. When we got home, we stayed as far away from each other as we could. We both knew that if we even brushed past each other we would tear each other's clothes off, and have raw, animal sex, right on the floor! The fire and desire was just that intense.

A few nights later, Hermes had taken it as long as he could. We were both sitting on the couch pretending to be watching a movie. I was staring at the screen, but I couldn't tell you what the movie was about. Hermes sat stiffly next to me and I could tell he wasn't focused on the movie, either. Finally, he turned to me and looked me dead in the eyes.

"Cynthia, I know you dated my brother, but I can't help it. I'm really feeling you." I returned his bold stare and whispered, "I'm feeling you too." Hermes grabbed me in his arms and stuck his tongue deep down my throat and I sucked on it hard! The lovemaking we shared that night wasn't sweet. It was rough and nasty. We fell to the floor and Hermes unzipped his pants and pulled out one of the biggest, stiffest cocks I had ever seen. He jerked my skirt up and ripped my panties off, as he pushed his penis into me hard. I screamed out, in pain and pleasure! Hermes roughly grabbed my butt cheeks and fucked me fast and hard. I was insane with pleasure! Finally, we both reached our peak and Hermes pumped a load of sperm into me. It was so good and we both came, howling like animals! It was shamefully intense and I knew that my life had forever changed in that one encounter. Sex with Hermes marked the beginning of a very deep, twenty-year relationship.

After that first sexual encounter, Hermes started having serious concerns about dating me. I had been in a relationship with his baby brother and even though he really cared about me, he felt like he had betrayed his brother. I eased his concerns by telling him how Roberto would come around for a few days and then disappear, with no explanation. Then I said, "I found out Roberto had a girlfriend, and a child, so at that point whatever relationship we had was clearly over. Besides, he'll be in jail for over 30 years. How can anybody wait that long?" Hermes nodded his head in agreement, and from that point on, he relaxed and allowed our relationship to grow.

It was October of 1994, and Hermes gave me a birthday party at 'Shooters on the Water', the same restaurant Roberto had taken me to. There were about twenty people with us and Hermes picked up the tab for everyone. My friends were looking at me and I could tell they were thinking, "Cynthia has really hit the jackpot with this one." I totally agreed.

Hermes was a quiet, soft-spoken man. He was attentive and knowledgeable, nurturing and caring, just like his brother and I was in heaven. Once we started hanging out, we were inseparable. All we wanted to do was spend time with each other. Hermes didn't go out or talk much on the phone and he had family in the states, but he rarely talked to them. The only person that would come to our apartment was his son Nathan and that was never a pleasant experience. He was so quiet and withdrawn, because his mother had told him horrible things about his dad, so he didn't trust him. Aside from his son, it was just Hermes and I alone for an entire year.

Hermes hated that I worked for eleven black attorneys. He would drop me off at work, and get pissed off if one of the attorneys spoke to me. He would always kiss me and tell me to be careful, because he knew I was in the building with nice, professional black men, all day. When it was quitting time, Hermes would be furious if I came out even a few minutes late. He would always ask, "So, what were you doing, that you couldn't come out on time?" and I would laugh and give him a big kiss.

What he didn't realize was, once I met him, no other man mattered to me. Hermes had me hooked and I wasn't going anywhere. He was just that good to me.

For that year, Hermes and I did everything together and we had sex at least twice a day. He was the best lover I ever had. After our first, raw sexual experience, Hermes slowed it down. He would always caress me so gently and he showed me how to take my time with him. Hermes had no restrictions in bed, except anal sex. He said he didn't want to defile me. Hermes taught me how to connect with my feelings during sex, and how to connect with him. He would kiss me everywhere and I would do the same thing to him. I can feel him, even as I write this and I realize that Hermes had sexually possessed me.

We moved into an apartment in Shaker Heights, a very nice area in the suburbs of Cleveland. We fixed our apartment up really nice, with expensive, quality things. Hermes said he had never done that before and then he shared something very profound with me.

"I want to put you in a position where you never have to depend on anyone, for anything, ever again."

I was floored! No one had ever cared for me like that, not even my own family! He immediately put his money where his mouth was. He asked me why I wasn't in college and I told him that I didn't have the money to go back. Hermes had me enroll, and paid all of my tuition. He would drive me to class, and pick me up after. In fact, there was nowhere I went that Hermes didn't drive me.

Sundays were our relaxation days. We would lie on the couch and watch TV. I would curl up in front of him, and he would pull me in close to him, wrap his arms around me and we would both fall asleep. I was so in love with him and it was hard for me to leave him or do anything without him. I had such a connection with him. I wanted to be with him every single moment of every day and he felt the same way about me.

If Hermes had to go out of town for business, he would always come back on the last plane that same day, so that he wouldn't have to spend the night away from me. One time he needed to stay in New York overnight, so he sent for me to come and join him. He refused to be apart from me a single night, so I hopped a plane and went to New York. When I got to the airport, Hermes picked me up in a white BMW 740i with white leather seats. That car was beautiful and very, very clean. That night we had a great time. We stayed in a beautiful hotel and he treated me to a wonderful dinner. It was only one night, but it felt like a mini vacation. Hermes always did everything in style. When we got back home, I told all my friends about it and they were so jealous. I had something that most women will never experience, a man that loved me, and had a lot of money! I felt really special until it all came to a screeching, halt.

Chapter Five
"Paradise Lost"

*"And ever has it been known that love knows
not its own depth until the hour of separation." - Khalil
Gibran* [7]

I can still remember that awful day like it was
yesterday. It was one year after Hermes and I met. He
got up that morning and told me that he had to go to
Detroit to take care of some business. Apparently, that
trip was supposed to be the most important trip of his
life. He was putting together a business deal that would
net him, twenty million dollars! When it was done, he
was going to retire so that he and I could enjoy the rest
of our lives together.

Hermes had been on many business trips, so I
shouldn't have been so stressed out. I should have been
happy about the money he was going to make, and his
plans to retire, but for some reason I couldn't. I had a
real bad feeling about this trip and I couldn't shake it. I
told him my feelings and begged him not to go.

"Please, Hermes! Don't go! I got a real bad feeling about this trip!"

I tried everything to persuade him. I piled up chairs and boxes at the door, trying to barricade it so he couldn't leave. It didn't matter what I said or what I did. Hermes was determined to go. I remember having a real cold feeling shoot through my body as he walked out the door. He kissed me and told me not to worry, and that he'd be back real soon. I didn't take his advice and when he left, I fell apart. I nervously paced the floor and tried to watch TV to relax, but I just couldn't shake that eerie feeling.

As the hours passed, I really started to panic. I hadn't received a single call from Hermes and that definitely wasn't like him. We were inseparable and whenever we had to part, we would call each other non-stop. This time, an entire day passed without a single call from Hermes. I called his phone over and over again, but he never picked up. As the evening came, I knew in my heart that something really bad had happened.

The clock continued to tick as I paced the floor all night, unable to sleep. Bright and early the next morning, I got the call. Federal enforcement agents in Michigan caught Hermes with 4.5 million dollars, and 1000 kilos of cocaine. I was devastated! I didn't know all of the details, but I knew that Hermes was in some very serious trouble!

I never knew the magnitude of Hermes's drug dealing. He was always at home with me and he rarely talked on the phone. The only time he left was when he went out of town for business and he was never gone for more than a day. I was really naïve, because I didn't feel threatened or uncomfortable with his lifestyle. I had never been around people who sold drugs and if I was, I didn't know about it. I was lulled into complacency by Hermes' love and money and my greatest delusion was that it would never end. That type of lifestyle doesn't last long and in most cases it comes to a tragic end. If Hermes had not been caught, he might have been killed or maimed and it never occurred to me, but I might have been in danger too. It was a tragic situation and I was numb with pain. It was clearly the worst day of my life!

Hermes finally called me collect from jail. When I heard his voice, I broke down crying. For a year, this man had been everything to me and now I had to face the prospect of losing him for a very, very long time. I was devastated and I didn't know how I was going to get through it. Hermes was my soul mate, and the love of my life. He had treated me like a queen, and taught me I was valuable and someone to be treasured. None of my other boyfriends had ever done that.

I was bawling and losing control when Hermes said in a stern voice, "Cynthia, stop crying. You got to be strong!" His powerful voice calmed me down a bit and I was able to listen to what he was saying to me. Hermes told me that he had an attorney that was defending all of his associates and that I shouldn't worry. He said that everything would be ok and though I told him I believed him, I really didn't. We both knew this was a game changer and our lives would never be the same. After we said our goodbyes, I hung up the phone and crumbled to the floor in tears! My perfect life was over and I hoped, without hope, that some miracle would happen and that my baby, my Hermes, would come back to me.

After I cried for what seemed like days, I got up off the floor, and sat down on the couch to think. The first thing that came to me was that Hermes would have to have good legal council. I didn't trust this attorney that was representing everybody. Hermes needed someone that was only working for him, someone that we could trust. The first name that came to mind was my old friend, John Wilson. He was an expert on searches and seizures, so I asked him as a personal favor to me, to assist with the case. John won me as a friend for life, when he agreed to help. I took John to meet Hermes. After talking to him, Hermes knew that John knew what he was talking about, so he hired him to help with the case.

Hermes was so upset during this time. He had been caught with 4.5 million dollars, but when the feds reported it to the bureau, they claimed they only found 2.5 million dollars. The Feds had stolen two million dollars of his money and Hermes was livid! It didn't matter, because he would soon find out that the justice system would end up taking all his money.

I had no idea that these kinds of cases dragged on so long. Hermes' case began in June of 1995 and it was delayed until October of 1996! I was so stressed, that I could barely function. It was bad enough Hermes had gotten caught and was in jail, but now I had to deal with not knowing the outcome. After doing some research, I got sick on my stomach. Hermes could be sentenced to so many years that I would be really old, or maybe dead by the time he got out. My greatest challenge was to keep my mind off the dire possibilities, and to keep it focused on a possible miracle. That was very hard. There was no doubt that Hermes had been caught red handed with the drugs and the money so he couldn't plead not guilty. He was going to do some time. Our only hope was that his attorney and John Wilson would work it out with the judge, to get him a reduced sentence. So, we all waited for the case to end, and the judge to announce Hermes' fate.

In October of 1996, Hermes was ushered into the courtroom. I sat in the section behind him and my heart ached from the pressure of missing him. He turned and looked at me and his eyes bore a hole through my soul. He had been gone a year and five months and he had just as much of a hold on me, as if he had just made love to me that same morning. He was a part of me and no court case could tear us apart.

The judge walked into the courtroom and everyone was commanded to rise. My legs felt like boiled noodles, and I could barely stand up on them. The judge looked at Hermes and asked him if he had anything to say. "No, your honor." Hermes said, with a surprisingly calm voice. The judge looked straight at him and with cold, lifeless eyes, pronounced his sentence

"Mr. Montana, you have two choices. If you keep the 2.5 million dollars, you will be sentenced to forty years in federal prison. Or, if you relinquish your claim to the 2.5 million dollars, you will be sentenced to fourteen years in federal prison. Take a few minutes to think about it, Mr. Montana."

Hermes turned and looked at me. His eyes said, "What should I do?" For me, there was no question about it. I yelled, "Hermes, forget the money! I can't live without you for forty years!" Tears welled up in his eyes as he turned to the judge and said, "Your Honor, I'll give up my rights to the money."

"Very well. Mr. Hermes Montana, I sentence you to fourteen years in federal prison with all rights to the 2.5 million dollars, relinquished." The judge hammered the gavel, and told the guards to take Hermes away from me. I ran to him and he turned and grabbed me and we clung to each other for as long as we could. Then, the guards pulled Hermes away, and ushered him out of the courtroom. I stood there, frozen. I had two different mindsets. On the one hand, Hermes didn't get sentenced to forty years. That would have been the end of his life, and mine. For that, I was grateful. But, I still had to face the reality that Hermes would be gone for over a decade! By the time he got out things would be totally different. It didn't matter, because the one thing that would never change was my love for Hermes, and that would sustain me for the fourteen years.

Chapter Six
"Survival"

"If you don't like something, change it.
If you can't change it, change your attitude. Don't
complain."
Maya Angelou [8]

After the court ordeal, I went back to our apartment with a new resolve. Just knowing the outcome made it easier for me to get centered. Before he was sentenced it was hard to get a handle on things, because I didn't know what was going to happen. Now that I knew, I could prepare, and make a game plan for my survival.

Hermes was moved from the Wayne County Federal Prison to a detention center in Milan Michigan, because he was a vegetarian. Milan was about two and a half hours from where I lived, but I decided that seeing Hermes on a regular basis was my top priority. During the week I would take care of my business and on the weekend, my release and relaxation was to drive the two and a half hours to see Hermes. I would talk to him on the phone all the way to the detention center, and all the way back home again. In spite of it all, Hermes and I still had an incredible bond.

What's Done in the Dark...

As fate would have it, there was a guy in Hermes' section of the detention center who knew me. I used to mess around with him when I lived on Martin Luther King, back when Allison and I would have our wild parties. There was no attachment between us. We would meet occasionally for casual sex and that was the extent of our relationship. I reconnected with him when Hermes and I moved into our new apartment in Shaker Heights. I only talked to him a few times on the phone. Now, the crazy thing was, this guy's cousin was also in the center with Hermes and he confirmed that we had a thing going on. I couldn't believe it! It wasn't true and of course I denied it, but Hermes kept ragging me about it for years.

It was really hard dealing with Hermes in jail. He was a dictator like Fidel Castro or Rafael Trujillo. But, the truth is, I kind of liked his take-charge attitude. He was so frustrated that he couldn't control his situation, or me. Hermes took the separation really hard and he always felt like the victim. I felt like a victim too, because I was hurting for what I had lost. I was also hurting for Hermes, and his pain.

Hermes went to the 'hole' a lot in prison, because he wanted peace and separation from the general population. He would start a fight on purpose so the guards would take him to the hole as punishment. He would be in isolation, away from everyone and that's exactly what he wanted. It was an incredibly hard time and when I look back on it, I realize that only God carried me through it.

Hermes's incarceration affected every area of my life. One of my big issues was my education. Hermes had paid my tuition before he went to jail and I was afraid that I'd have to quit school, because I had no money.

With Hermes in jail, I figured I couldn't depend on him for money, but I was wrong. When I told him my dilemma, he said not to worry. He would keep paying my tuition, so I could graduate. He had money stashed and he told me where it was. He also had people bring money to me. After it was all said and done, he had stashed a little over two million dollars in CASH! I was shocked! Not only did Hermes pay for my tuition, he also gave me a monthly allowance. That's when I really found out how financially smart Hermes was. He had a lot of money saved, so he was able to allot money to me so that I could live comfortably while he was gone. Hermes gave me $2,500 for bills, and spending money for clothes, entertainment, etc. He also bought me a jeep. So, the man that had taken good care of me when he was with me, continued to provide for me while he was gone. I had never had a man that handled his business like that. Hermes had his faults certainly, but he knew what it meant to be a man to his woman and I so miss that!

In December of 1997, I graduated from college with a BA in Business Administration with a major in Accounting. I wish I could say that everything went great after that, but I can't. I really thought that when I graduated people would be knocking down my door, to offer me jobs. I was wrong. What I realized was that the market was flooded with college graduates and without connections, I was competing against hundreds of college graduates for very limited jobs. When I finally got a position, they offered me the same amount of money that I was making before I got my degree. I couldn't believe it! I was so depressed and I was even more grateful for the help I was getting from Hermes. He was my ace in the hole and I adored him!

Stepping Out

I was frustrated with the economy and the state of the job market, so I "pulled myself up by my bootstraps" and I started my own business. I named it, 'Cynthia and

Company', and I solicited business from my large base of personal and business relationships. I started out preparing income taxes and I was doing well. Shortly after that, I got a call from a headhunter. They offered me an accounting job at a private company, where the wife was giving up her position to stay at home with her children. The owners really liked me, so they groomed me to take over her position and they gave me a new job title, 'Director of Accounting'.

One of the best times of my life was when I worked for that company. I made great money and they also paid me to work for one of their other businesses. We had a blast! Not only did they pay me well and give me a respected position, but they also made working there, fun. We regularly traveled for business and the company would pick up the tab. One time we went to New York for business and we stayed at the Marriott Marquis Midtown. It was a fabulous hotel and they really rolled out the red carpet for us. That night, we all went down to the restaurant to eat, but before we ordered dinner we had double shots of 1800 Tequila. I hadn't eaten all day and I was downing the double shots on an empty stomach. I ended up running out to the bathroom to throw up and I threw up all night, and the next day at the airport. When our plane finally got in, they had to escort me home, because I was still so sick. I will never forget that experience and after that, I have never downed alcohol on an empty stomach, ever!

I worked that job from 1998 to 2005, but I was still working my own business, doing taxes. My business was growing and I made the decision to quit my job and work my own business, full time. I really wanted to see if I could support myself. Hermes and I had planned to go to his home in the Dominican Republic, once he was released from prison and I wanted to keep my accounting firm in the states, and possibly open one in the Dominican Republic. So, I gave my job notice, and prepared to work my own business. My job had depended on me a lot and I didn't want to leave them hanging, so I gave them a nine-month notice. They had been good to me and I wanted to give them all the time they needed to transition someone into my position. My boss was so grateful, that he gave me a $5,000 parting gift! That's the kind of people that they were and I missed them when I left.

The Long Haul

Meanwhile, I was still dealing with Hermes in jail. I became his everything and we talked everyday. If he needed money, I sent it to him, because, I had his two million dollars. I even started forming a bond with his son, Nathan. If he needed cleats, I bought them. Whatever Nathan needed, I took care of it. I would always send pictures of him to Hermes. I really felt bad for his son, because he had to deal with his father going away a second time. Before, the sentence was five years and now it was fourteen. I always talked positive about Hermes to Nathan, because he had never heard anything but bad things about him from his mother. I wanted to change that perception.

Nathan came to a crossroads when he went to Benedictine School. His mother would take the money for his school expenses, and spend it. To put a stop to it, Hermes paid the school directly through me, of course. He was a good father and paid over and above what he was supposed to pay. Out of spite, Nathan's mother took him out of the good school, and put him into a public school in Shaker Heights. I couldn't believe it. What mother would take her son from a good, encouraging school environment, to a school where the students were unmotivated, and the teachers were ineffective. Sure enough, it had a negative effect on Nathan. He started smoking weed and almost didn't graduate. I called around to find tutors for him, but no one from his family would help me, not his mother, his grandmother, his aunts, no one. Hermes and I were the only ones that cared about his education and we wanted to make sure he graduated.

There was an opportunity for Nathan to go to Hampton for the summer. It was a great program, so we made sure that he went. He did so well, that I persuaded Hermes to send him to Hampton during the normal school year. Nathan went, but after the first year he got caught changing the grades on his report card. The school gave him another chance, but it was a big blow for us.

When Nathan came home for summer break, he stayed with me. Hermes thought it was best and I agreed. His mother never cared what happened to him and if he lived with me he might have a fighting chance. We both had high hopes, but things started going sour as soon as Nathan got to my house. He would lie about everything. For example, he told us he was working. Everyday he would leave the house like he was going to work, but the crazy thing was, he really didn't have a job. He also announced that he wasn't going back to school at Hampton. Everyday, Nathan would smoke marijuana. He was high all the time. He wasn't in school, he wasn't working, and he was just sitting around smoking weed and I had enough! I told Hermes that Nathan had to move or pay money to live with me. We both agreed he had to go.

Once he was on his own, Nathan's life began to spiral downward, fast! He was roaming the streets all day, high as a kite. One fateful day, he went in a fast food restaurant where he had previously worked, and robbed it. It was crazy, because he had to know that everyone working there knew him. They all testified that Nathan pointed a nine-millimeter gun in three of the employee's faces. It was loaded with 16 rounds. That meant ten years for each person! The ironic thing is he never got to spend the $425 he stole. He took it to a friend's house and asked him to keep it so he wouldn't get caught with it. His friend stole the money. Nathan lost all of his clothes too. He took them to another 'so-called' friend's house and they kept all his clothes. No one knows what happened to the gun. He wouldn't tell anyone what he did with it.

Nathan planned to run away and hide from the law, but I convinced him to turn himself in. It was only a matter of time before the police caught him and it would be much worse if they did. So, he agreed and I hired John Wilson to represent him.

When it was time for Nathan to turn himself in, he didn't. He just kept going and hanging out at a different friend's house everyday. He needed money, so one day he went to the local university, and tried to steal a radio from a car. Of course, he got caught and once again, Wilson was brought in to represent him in court. If it were not for Wilson having a good relationship with the judge, Nathan would have gotten the maximum sentence of 30 years in prison. Instead he was only sentenced to six years, three years for the gun, and three years for the robbery.

I was really devastated when Nathan went to jail. I had embraced him like the son I never had, but I had lost him to the streets and then to the legal system. Actually Nathan' situation was the culmination of a life of let downs for me. As a young girl I was devastated by my parent's drug addiction. I saw how it deteriorated their bodies and set them on a course to live a really low life, way below their talent and abilities. Then, when I grew up I was disappointed with the way life turned out for me. I hadn't achieved my goals and I was stuck in a rut that I didn't know how to get out of. Then Hermes showed up and turned it all around for me. He was truly my knight in shining armor, until it all came tumbling down. To say that I was depressed was an understatement.

During this time my parents separated, and my mother's addiction really escalated. When I look back on it, I'm amazed at how my mom was able to support herself, my sister and me, with her accounting jobs. She would finish her work, and then get high. That was her routine. Every minute that she wasn't working, she was getting high. I remember the deep shame that I felt when my mom would go to the dope house to buy drugs. My friends would call me and say, "I just saw your mom on Tuscora Street". That was the street where everyone bought drugs.

"Cynthia, you mama looks bad. You better tell her to stop getting high," as if I never tried to stop her. I would ask my mother if she was buying drugs and she would always deny it. I remember having really heated arguments with my mom about her drugs.

Eventually my mother's need for drugs outweighed what she could afford, so she started writing bad checks all over the place to pay for the drugs. It finally caught up with her, and she was caught and sentenced to six months in state prison. She didn't go to jail right away, because she hired my friend, Attorney Wilson to represent her. He was initially able to get her probation. That didn't work out, because my mother kept violating the probation by writing bad checks. She got caught so many times that Wilson couldn't help her anymore, so she was eventually sentenced to the six months in prison. When my mother's case first started, she begged Wilson not to tell me, but once she was sentenced there was no way that he could hide it.

When I heard the news, I was really hurt and scared for my mom. I was also worried about my sister, because with my mother gone she had to stay with my dad. His addiction was so bad, that he couldn't keep a place to live. He and my sister moved constantly from house to house. It worried me so much that I had to see a shrink about it. I only went once and the advice he gave me was really good, but in reality, I needed more that just a one time visit. I had never really dealt with the pain of being raised with two dope addicts. I dealt with Hermes's incarceration and then Nathan's. Then my mother gets locked up for six months, while my heroin addicted father is dragging my sister from house to house! My God, it's a wonder I didn't lose my mind! I dealt with it by acting like it wasn't really happening. I would internalize each problem as it came and I kept it moving.

Fortunately for me, my business was going well. I was reputable, and making six figures because of referrals. I always felt responsible for my family and I did my best to take care of my mother while she was in prison. I sent her clothes, boxes of food, and money. I also kept her business in order, as best I could. I even filed her taxes with her direction, of course. The day my mother got out of jail, my grandfather and I picked her up. I had found her an attic apartment and I paid her rent six months in advance. We moved all her stuff in, and arranged her apartment so it would be comfortable for her. I also bought her a little car to get around in. She was so happy and surprised that I could do as much as I did. What she didn't understand was, I was blessed by God's grace. That's why I was able to help my family and find contentment.

In the Meantime...

During the six years that Nathan was in prison, he really acted out. He started fighting and was always in trouble for something. I hated it, but for Hermes's sake I had to be there for him. Everyone had abandoned him, including his mother. I made sure that he had everything he needed. I kept money on his books and made sure he got his yearly clothing box with sweats, jogging suits, and other necessities. He had a TV, CD's, and money. I also bought him a lot of positive books to keep his mind right. I wanted him to focus on the fact that there was a big world outside and that he would one day be going back to it. One of the books I gave Nathan to read was about a man that had gotten out of prison, and went on to become a successful chef. I wanted to remind him that there was life outside of jail and that he could do anything he wanted with his life. Nathan was smart kid. He was a business major in school and I told him that when he got out he could take over my accounting business in Cleveland, because I was going to live in the Dominican Republic. Hermes was giving me the directives, because he really loved his son. He felt so bad. He felt like he let his son down. I did all I could to try to help Nathan, and to help ease Hermes' guilt. He had so much pain, because he felt that he had not always been there for his son.

I was getting bored with just working and taking care of Hermes and I needed an outlet. One day, while I was at Cleveland State I saw a flyer about salsa dancing. After all the pain and stress in my life I thought dancing might be a good outlet for me, so I tried it. I met a girl who taught me all the steps and I started going to the club with her and another friend. At the club, I met a gay guy named Monty who really embraced me. He taught me all the intricate moves, how to maneuver the turns, and how to move my arms and legs. I became really good at dancing the Salsa. It became a big part of my life and I would go to the club every Wednesday, Friday, and Saturday. I met all the other people who were regulars at the club and soon we became one big, happy dance family. We would meet at Monty's house, then all go out to eat before we went to the club. Then, after the club we would finish the party at Monty's house. I started dancing Salsa in 1995 and I'm still dancing it today. Of course, I didn't tell Hermes about it, because I knew he would've had a fit!

Eight years after I met Monty he died from Aids. That was another big source of pain for me. He asked for me when he was dying and I went to the hospital. He couldn't even speak. I was so hurt, because we had become so close. We all had so much fun together and the loss of Monty hit us all really hard.

Time Served

The years seemed to zoom by and after six years Nathan was released from prison. I was staying with my mother at the time to save money, so when Nathan got released he came to stay with me at my mother's house. He needed to go on job interviews, so I bought him nice clothes and other stuff so he didn't feel like he had to rob somebody to get what he needed. I also wanted to get him an apartment and help him get his license back, but Hermes wanted me to give Nathan the money, so he could take care of his own business. I knew that wouldn't work. I really believed that he needed somebody to show him what to do. I could also feel that things were not quite right with Nathan. He was acting like he was ok and that he wanted to get on with his life, but I could feel there was something else going on. One warm summer night it all came to a head.

Nathan was really interested in learning about his Dominican culture. So I thought, 'What better way to learn about the Dominican culture than to learn to dance the Salsa, a Dominican favorite?' So one night I took Nathan to the club. All of my friends were there and we were all having a really good time when everything came to a screeching halt. With no warning and no encouragement from me, Nathan hit me on the butt! It wasn't the kind of tap where you're excited at a game or when you hit a child playfully on the butt to go to bed. It felt like a tap of ownership like he was saying, "You're mine". I was shocked. I leaned over and told him that if he ever hit me like that on the butt again, I would hurt him. From that point on, the evening started to go downhill. It was getting late so I decided that it was time to go. As we were walking to the car Nathan started harassing a man that walked past us. The man was minding his own business, when Nathan yelled out, "What you lookin' at me for? You want some of me?" Nathan ran up to the man and started pushing and pulling on him. He was all hyped up and acting really crazy. I had never seen him like that and I had known him since he was 10 years old. At that point, he started yelling in the man's face, "Don't nobody mess with me!" It got so bad I had to call his mother and I never talked to her. She had always hated me because I was dating Hermes. When I got her on the line, I yelled to Nathan, "Nathan, your mother is on the phone!" He stopped immediately, and came to the phone. After talking to his mother, he started to calm down and I made up my mind to drive him home to stay with his mother.

While I was driving to his mother's house, Nathan was begging me to take him home with me. He was really close to my family, and under normal circumstances; I would have taken him with me. But this time I just couldn't. I really needed time to process what was happening with him, and what was happening with me. When I finally dropped him off I went home and broke down. I cried and cried. It hurt me so bad. I couldn't believe that Nathan would feel on me and disrespect me the way he did. It was horrible and I was glad he was with his mother. I didn't want to deal with him.

Chapter Seven
"The Dog Days of Captivity"
"Life isn't about waiting for the storm to pass, it's about learning to Dance in the Rain."
Vivian Green [9]

Hermes was doing his time and getting on my nerves. Every day he was calling me with something to do and expected me to carry it out to the letter. When he first went to jail, the first thing he told me to do was to get a Cell Phone. "Cynthia, you got to get a Cell Phone! I can't put up with you not answering my calls!" He was so demanding and as soon as I bought the phone, it never stopped ringing. Hermes called me constantly with all kinds of demands, "Do this and do that" and it was usually little things. But, one day Hermes asked me to do something that I never thought he would. That particular day I went to visit him in really good spirits. It was a pretty day and I felt good. When I saw Hermes, I smiled real big. I walked up to him and gave him a warm hug, and a big, juicy kiss. Immediately, I felt his body tense up. I stepped back and looked at Hermes and I could see that he wasn't in the mood to play. "Sit down, Cynthia", he quietly said. "I got something serious to talk about." I sat down. Hermes moved in close to me and whispered in my ear, "Cynthia, I need you to bring me some weed." I was thinking, 'Did he just ask me to bring marijuana to the jail?'

"Cynthia, did you hear me? The next time you come bring me some weed. I got to make some money while I'm in here." Puzzled, I replied,

"But Hermes, they search me when I come in. How can I bring drugs in here without getting caught?" Then Hermes shocked me.

"It's easy", he casually replied as he leaned in closer. "All you have to do is put some weed in a little Ziploc bag. Then, put a knot in it and stick it up in your pussy."

"What?" I asked, rather loudly.

"Shhh! Be quiet. You can do this. They won't know you got it. The machines can't pick it up when it's in you. Then, when you get in here go to the bathroom and take the bag out."

I couldn't believe my ears. This was by far the worst thing that Hermes had ever asked me to do. What if I got caught? Not only would Hermes be in jail, I would too! I really didn't want to do it, but I did. The truth is, I could never say no to Hermes. I loved him just that much.

After the visit I was shaken to the core. I went home and cried my eyes out. Of all the things that Hermes had asked me to do, he had never asked me to risk my life for him. I just couldn't believe he would put me in that position. After crying it out and thinking it through, I realized that Hermes did still love me. Maybe somebody was threatening him. I didn't know, but in my heart of hearts I truly believed that Hermes would never ask me to do something so dangerous if he really didn't need it. So, I dried my tears, and started working on a plan to help him. Just like he said, it seemed easy enough getting the marijuana into the jail, but how was I going to get it into Hermes's hands? Suddenly it came to me! Every time I went to see him I would buy him a bag of popcorn from the concession stand in the visitor's area. Hermes loved popcorn, and all the guards and the inmates were used to seeing me give it to him. I realized that the popcorn would make the perfect cover. I could put the marijuana in the bag of popcorn and hand it to Hermes, and he could eat it along with the popcorn. It was perfect and with my plan in place, I felt empowered. I calmed down and went over the plan over and over again in my mind, until I had it down pat. Then I stretched out on my bed and sleep came immediately.

Partners in Crime

When the day came for me to visit Hermes, I was a nervous wreck! I was sure one of the guards would look at me and know I was a criminal, too. Shaking all over I went through the security check. Walking slowly with a huge knot in my throat, I almost fainted when the guard said, "You're good." Whew! Thank God Hermes knew what he was talking about. Now, with my biggest hurdle behind me I confidently walked to the concession stand and bought a bag of popcorn. I was calm and I even made small talk with the clerk. After paying for the popcorn, I smoothly glided to the bathroom and went to the last stall. Just as Hermes had instructed me, I pulled the plastic bag filled with the marijuana out of my vagina. I purposely left a little of my dew glistening on the bag as I dropped it in the popcorn. When I came out of the bathroom I felt an adrenaline rush as I spotted Hermes. As calmly as I could, I walked over to him and gave him a big hug and kiss. Hermes whispered in my ear, "Did you do it?" I smiled big and ever so slightly nodded my assent. I was relieved as I handed over the bag of popcorn. It was finally out of my hands!

Hermes and I sat down, and tried to make small talk. It was hard. We both knew that at any time a guard could come over and inspect the bag. Hermes smelled the popcorn and smiled, sheepishly. He could smell my scent in the bag. Being a master at controlling his emotions, he looked normal as he munched on the popcorn. He pursed his lips as if he was munching on my sweet spot and then, winked at me. I felt the blood rush to my face. I was inflamed with lust! Hermes was my man and even in jail he knew how to set me off. I almost climaxed, as he slowly licked and munched the kernels. Finally, I saw a big lump in Hermes's throat as he swallowed another handful of popcorn and I knew that he had also swallowed the bag of marijuana. I was amazed, as Hermes it all gulped down. He breathed a deep breath out, and continued to talk calmly to me as if nothing had happened. When he finished the popcorn I breathed a deep sigh of relief, because the marijuana was out of the bag and no one could prove that I had brought it in. Later, Hermes would go to the toilet and eliminate the bag of marijuana, then divide it up to sell to the inmates. Later, I would also go to the bathroom and with my own fingers I would feverishly finish the climax that Hermes had started!

On a Roll

Bringing in the weed became routine to me and after the first couple of times I lost my nervousness. Then one day Hermes kicked it up a notch. I came to see him, just like any other day. After he swallowed the weed in the popcorn, he leaned in close and whispered in my ear,

"Cynthia, mail me a box of baby powder and put the weed down in the middle of the box. It's easier that way."

By this time, I trusted that Hermes knew what he was talking about, so I did exactly what he said. After my visit, I stopped at a drugstore and bought the baby powder along with some other toiletries. Then, I stopped off and bought the drugs. As soon as I got home I pulled the top off of the baby powder, and put the drugs deep in the middle of it. Then, I put the top back on it, put it in a box, and positioned the other toiletries around it. After sealing up the box, I headed to the post office to mail it to Hermes. I wanted to do it quickly, before I started having second thoughts.

I was nervous as the clerk at the post office weighed the box, and told me how much the postage was. I asked for express shipping so Hermes would get it the next day. I couldn't stand to wait for days to see if he got it. The sad thing is, I was risking my life every time I went to see Hermes. Now, I was adding more risk by sending drugs through the mail. If I got caught I knew I would be charged with a felony, and locked up for a long time. Even though I knew the risk, I was under Hermes's spell and I did exactly what he instructed me to do.

There's an old saying that, 'Eventually, the chickens come home to roost.' What that means is, whatever you put out good or bad, is going to eventually return to you, and my situation was no exception. As soon as I got comfortable mailing the drugs to Hermes, the worst thing that could happen did. Hermes sold drugs to an inmate that turned out to be an informant and as soon as Hermes made the transaction, the inmate reported it to the authorities. Before Hermes had time to contact me to tell me what had happened, I had already mailed my next package. When the box of toiletries arrived, the guards searched the box with a fine-toothed comb. They found the drugs and of course I was picked up. My fingerprints were all over the box of baby powder! As I mentioned earlier, I had been arrested years before for shoplifting, so I had a record. Now, I was being charged with another felony! To say that I was in a panic is an understatement. I freaked out, because I really didn't have any defense. It was clear that I had mailed Hermes the marijuana, so I didn't have a leg to stand on. I couldn't believe I would actually be going to prison! I wasn't like Hermes and his brother, and a lot of the other people who were locked up. I had no experience being in jail, especially prison and I knew I couldn't survive in that environment.

Just as they were about to start the court proceedings, Hermes totally shocked me, and my attorney. He negotiated a deal with the district attorney to have nine months added to his sentence so he could do the time, for my crime. He definitely didn't have to do that. Even though he asked me to bring him the drugs, I could've said, "No". On my own I took part in the illegal action and Hermes had no obligation to help me, but he did! My love for Hermes skyrocketed, because thanks to him I was free! If I never knew that he loved me, then I knew for sure. They tried to take me off of Hermes's visitors list, but being his intelligent, persuasive self, Hermes persuaded them to put me back on. That's one thing I was certain of, Hermes knew how to get things done.

The extra nine months were a blow to both of us, but we shook it off, and did the best we could to deal with it. Hermes was sent to a prison in Atlanta, and one of his cronies from New York named Foster, was in jail with him. His wife Veronica was from Florida and I would coordinate my visits with hers so could share the hotel, and give each other support. It was so sad and stressful, and so hard to deal with for all of us.

Hermes had enough with the conflicts and stress of being in the general population, so he started acting out and creating a ruckus. The guards would drag him off to the hole where he would be totally alone. Most people would hate being in a small, confined space alone, but not Hermes. He got put in the hole on purpose. He preferred that, than dealing with the other inmates and their drama. Part of me was sad that Hermes was so alone, but another part of me was glad that he wasn't in danger.

Testing The Waters

I waited a long time for Hermes to be released and for three years I didn't date anybody. Then I started getting really lonely, and wondering if Hermes was the man for me. Eventually, I started dating other men and the first one was a Peruvian named Carlos. I had a really good time with Carlos, and he seemed to be a good guy until the day he randomly beat up a boy with a jackhammer! Apparently, the young boy had said something stupid to Carlos, so he pulled a jackhammer out of his truck, and beat the boy in the head with it. He beat him so bad, that he permanently messed up the boy's brain. Carlos was arrested and the state gave him two years in jail. Unfortunately, while he was in jail his green card expired and after living in the United States since he was two, Carlos was deported to Peru. He had been in America so long that he had no idea how to live in the Peru. It was a serious culture shock for Carlos and terrified, he tried to commit suicide. Fortunately, someone found him in time, and took him to the hospital. Even though they revived him, Carlos was never able to settle in to life in Peru. The last I heard, he was a heroin addict and I felt really bad for him.

After Carlos, I dated a man named, William. We called him Bi-William, because we thought he had been messing around with Monty when he was in the states. Aside from my suspicions about his sexual orientation, he also tried to pit me against my friend Allison and I couldn't deal with that. Our relationship ended quickly and I didn't care, because he really didn't mean anything to me.

I was on a roll with the dating thing and I quickly moved on to another guy named, Warren. He was a real estate agent and I handled his accounting. I don't know why I got with him. He was horrible in bed. He would just get on top of me, and pound me quick and hard, and then be done. He wouldn't even try to please me. I had to get rid of him, like I did the many other guys that weren't right for me.

Kenneth was a guy that had just come out of prison after doing 12 years for a drug charge. He was on house arrest at his mother's house for the last six months of his sentence. One day he came to my house to pick up his check, and he flirted with me. I thought he was cute, so I responded. Kenneth and I ended up dating for two years, right before Hermes was released from prison. I moved into Kenneth's house, because I didn't have to pay rent. I was being slick and trying to save some money, so I'd have a cushion for Hermes when he got out.

Kenneth and I discussed Hermes from the moment we met. I told him that he was satisfying my temporary need for a man, and that I was helping him adjust to being at home from jail. The mistake I made was staying with Kenneth until Hermes got out of jail. As soon as Hermes hugged me, he could feel the presence of another man. I confessed, because I knew that he knew. He forgave me, but not completely.

Chapter Eight
"Freedom"

*"Then came the healing time, hearts
started to shine, soul felt so fine,
oh what a freeing time it was."*
Aberjhani [10]

Hermes was finally released from jail and as expected, he was deported back to the Dominican Republic. When it was time for him to leave, I paid a Dominican government official to delete Hermes's deportation record. He did and Hermes didn't have to stand in the immigration line, or go through all the formalities that everyone else had to go through. He finally arrived in the Dominican Republic in November of 2006, and he arranged for me to fly in right away.

When Hermes got home, he expected a large sum of money waiting for him from his business profits. The years he was in the U.S. he had never taken any of the money that was generated from his business in the Dominican Republic. Hermes had a mansion and 1350 acres of farmland waiting for him when he got to the Dominican. The cattle on his farm provided milk to a fortune 500 American company. A mining company was also mining minerals on his property, which paid him thirteen to fifteen thousand dollars a month. Hermes also had racehorses, plus cattle that he sold to slaughterhouses. He was sure that his family had saved some of that massive amount of money, for him. What he found, was that his family had squandered all the money he earned. There was no money left and Hermes was enraged! The whole situation stirred up childhood issues that he had never dealt with. His mother had a one-night stand with his father, and she got pregnant with Hermes. His father never wanted to live with him or his mother and it wasn't until Hermes started making money that his father came on the scene, and decided to live with him. Considering the type of relationship Hermes had with his father, he probably shouldn't have trusted him with all his assets. But, it was too late and the only thing left to do was to salvage as much as he could.

It was really bad. His family had done no maintenance to the house and Hermes was disgusted to find out that the house was really damaged, with most of problems hidden by furniture. Most of the money that Hermes and I had was used to fix the house, and the other things that needed to be done. With all the expenses piling up, in a year all the money was gone. Hermes's father had taken out a second mortgage on the farm and it was in foreclosure. Thank God, Hermes was able to save it. The bank only charged him a percentage of what it was worth and he had the title switched back to his name. At that point, the only thing left to do was to put his father and brother out of the house, which he did. We were both elated to see them go!

Hermes and I were happy, in spite of the money issues, and problems with the property. We had been apart for years and we were just happy to be together. We spent days on end making love and pampering each other.

Hermes was finding ways to make money and I was working my virtual business, so over time we were able to create a really good life for ourselves. Hermes and I had beautiful dogs that we walked around the large property. We would take long drives along the ocean, and breathe in the fresh, ocean breezes. Hermes and I were in paradise.

Hermes was very possessive and he wanted me by his side, twenty-four seven. Even when he took a shower he would call me into the bathroom, and have me write down things he wanted to get done. Even though he was possessive, I didn't mind. In fact, that was one of the things I loved about him. Life had never been sweeter for us, until it all came crashing down!

As Fate Would Have It

Early in the morning in October 2008, I was talking to my best friend Sidney on the phone. Suddenly she yells out, "Cynthia, I just saw your face on the news!"

"What?" I replied. "What are you talking about?"

Sidney responded back, barely able to talk, "They just showed a caption. It said, Three Indicted for Mortgage Fraud!"

Sidney then told me that the news reporter said that I had run away to the Dominican Republic to escape justice. I was shocked! I immediately called Hermes, then my friend, Attorney Wilson. No one knew what was going on. Finally, Wilson found out that I was being indicted for preparing fake documents. Apparently, I was sent a subpoena in July of 2008 for client information, but I never received it. Wilson advised me to call the court and let them know that I was in the Dominican Republic, and that I had never received the subpoena. He also told me to tell them that I couldn't come back to the States. I believe that if I had gone back then, I would have been immediately indicted and jailed. What really happened was that a client of mine was buying houses and appraising them for high amounts of money, then taking the money out of them, but never paying the mortgages. I was the tax preparer for him and his client's taxes. They told the authorities that I was preparing fake documents for them. I knew then that I was in real bad trouble! I needed $50,000 for Wilson and Jeff to represent me, and of course, Hermes paid the money. Hermes was in a panic, because he didn't want me to leave.

"Cynthia, if you leave, you'll never come back. I don't trust those American courts. You have everything you need right here with me, so why go back? Your life is here with me!"

Hermes begged me to stay, but I knew that I couldn't. I had family in America, and it's where I was born. I couldn't imagine never being able to return to America. I knew it really hurt Hermes, but I had to go back to clear my name.

I left, and because I didn't have a house or car or anything, I went to live with my mother. I was sure that I would be back in the Dominican in a few months so staying with my mother wouldn't be such a big deal. I was so wrong. The case ended up dragging on for two years, and it was the worst two years of my life! I was constantly going to court, because I refused to say that I was guilty of something I didn't do. The judge held up my case for no reason, other than motives of his own.

In April 2009, Wilson and Jeff finagled a visit for me to the Dominican Republic, for six weeks. Hermes had moved out of our home and had moved to a residential resort community that we had always dreamed of living in. When I was living there, we would visit the resort on Sundays for brunch. Since I couldn't be there, I looked on the Internet to help Hermes find our house, and we finally settled on one that was perfect for us. When I got there in April, I moved into our new home and those six weeks were the best times of our lives. We would walk our two beautiful dogs, and enjoy our new home. After the six weeks, I had to go back to the states. That day was a very emotional one for both of us. In the airport, Hermes and I clung to each other, crying our eyes out. It was one of the worst days of my life, as I boarded the plane away from Hermes, and on to the court drama.

After I left, Hermes started thinking about his days as a drug lord, when he was "the Man" and had all the money that any man could hope for. His delusions of grandeur set him off on a negative spiral and he started selling drugs again. On his first trip, Hermes went to Spain to live for a while. He had just sold his mansion, and bought the new house, so I couldn't understand why he would want to live in Spain. He would call me for money, all the time. I was still working my virtual business, so I sent him whatever I could. Then, Hermes went to Ecuador, then back to Spain, and back to Ecuador. Hermes was getting really reckless and in December of 2009 he was jailed in Ecuador. He called me, because in Ecuador you can have whatever you want if you have money. He told me that he had $150,000 coming to Ecuador, but they confiscated it in the airport. I couldn't help Hermes. I didn't have any money. I was dealing with my own problems. They locked Hermes up in Ecuador for selling drugs.

Aside from what Hermes was dealing with, after years of going back and forth I was charged with creating fake documents, and sentenced to three years in jail! It was a state indictment and every news reporter in Cleveland was on the case. It was big, because it involved the Slavic Village area, a new community development project. Jeff and Wilson were in the court room when the verdict was read and Wilson started crying. I had never seen him like that. I couldn't respond at all, because I was in shock. I couldn't process that I would have to serve three years in jail! Wilson took my hand and said, "If I have to pull on every favor I've ever had, I'm going to get you out of here!" This is one time that I really needed Hermes.

Chapter Nine
"My Life is in Your Hands"
"Now I Know Why The Caged Bird Sings"
Maya Angelou [11]

When the day came for me to be escorted to jail, I was numb and clueless. I knew that I was not the kind of person that belonged in jail. I just wasn't from that kind of life. I knew that I had to do my best to survive. I tucked away my fears concerning my fate, and my fears and feelings for what Hermes was going through. I was in the county jail called, The Justice Center of Cleveland. Jeff filed a motion the next morning. The motion was for the judge to reconsider my sentence, or let me out to handle my affairs. The judge put a hold on me for seven and a half months. He extended the holds of two weeks, twelve times, so I wouldn't be shipped off to prison. Thank God for that!

County jail was something else. The Correctional Officers didn't care about anything or anyone. In that place I realized that anything could happen to you, at any time. The first person that I met when I got there was Mildred Dyson. She helped me to get situated. She tried to fill me in on the jail protocol, and the dos and don'ts of life in jail. I really appreciated her, because I had no clue how to act.

I was always an avid reader, and to pass the time, I read a lot of books. Reading helped me ignore all the craziness going on around me. I also went to church whenever I could. It's funny how I never thought about going to church until trouble hit. I think that's the way it is with a lot of us. The only time we give God attention is when we need His help. It's a good thing He's not petty. We only run to Him in times of need, but He's still there to help us.

I was surprised too, because the entire time I was in jail, nobody bothered me. Mind you, I'm small and petite; a likely candidate for abuse in jail, but surprisingly, it never happened. No lesbians approached me and no one challenged me to a fight.

At night, all kinds of crazy things would be going on, but I slept like a rock. My friend Mildred couldn't believe how I slept through the ruckus. I would be shocked nearly every morning when Mildred would tell me stories about who got beat up, and raped. It would be hard for me to believe, because I would never hear a thing. I slept all night, every night. It was amazing, because I could literally feel the arms of God rocking me like I was a baby! I would fall asleep so peacefully and I wouldn't wake up until it was time for breakfast.

The truly amazing thing is, not only did God help me sleep, he also gave me instructions on how to survive. Like one night, He told me to keep my eyes wide-open and pay attention and I promised Him I would. Honestly, it was such a surreal time for me.

In addition to Mildred, I also developed a relationship with a Nun named, Sister Margaret. She would come around a lot to get feedback on our living conditions, and to provide us with prayer when we needed it. I loved it when she came to visit, because I knew I could talk to her and that she really cared about what I had to say. She would take our concerns to the administration and sometimes they would actually address our issues. Sister Margaret was special and her prayers brought us all so much comfort.

Hermes really hurt me while I was jail. I would call him periodically and he would always rush me off the phone. He was never good at handling problems, unless the problem was something that money could fix. If it wasn't, he would depend on me to fix it. Hermes's money was definitely his strength. Without it, he was like a child.

A friend of ours from the Dominican came to town. When she came to visit me, I could've cried. It was so good to see a familiar face. She hugged me warmly and I could tell she was trying to hold back her tears. After sitting for a while, I could see her start to relax. Then she gave me the scoop about what was going on with Hermes and I couldn't believe it. Apparently, he had lost his mind, and started drinking. It was all a mystery to me, but I couldn't focus on him and his problems. Staying sane in jail was my only priority.

Freedom in a Box

On June, 2011, I received a court date and I was able to talk to the judge for the first time. Before I went into the courtroom Jason said, "Don't listen to anything the judge says. We're just trying to get you out of here. We can work on your case while you're out on probation." I did what Jeff told me to do. When it was my turn to talk to the judge, I told him all about myself, and what it was like for a person like me to be in the county jail. The judge listened patiently and after a few questions for my lawyer, he announced my sentence. As I stood up, my knees were shaking. I didn't know what to expect. After what had happened at my last sentencing, I couldn't predict what the judge was going to say.

"Cynthia Arroyo", he said, sternly. "I sentence you to five years of probation, three thousand community service hours, a $1,000 fine, $5,000 special fee and $222 in court costs."

When he finished, I breathed a huge sigh of relief! That meant I was finally out of the county jail! Thank you, Jesus! And surprisingly, I was out in an hour. Before we went to court, Jeff had filed my case and told my mother to pay all of my court costs. That way, when the judge gave the verdict, I could get out immediately. Once again, Hermes came to the rescue the only way he knew how. He had his assistant pay my fines and court costs, plus my five-year probation costs in advance, hoping that the court would cancel my probation, and let me go home to the Dominican.

When I got out, I was discombobulated. I had a bad taste in my mouth concerning accounting, because I realized I had no control over what other people were doing. I decided to change gears and some friends hired me at their law firm, as their legal secretary. I just needed to get my bearings back so I worked there four months, full-time.

Everything was going well until June of 2010, when I received a double whammy! The federal government was indicting me for the same charge as the state. I could not believe it! Jason was back on the case and with a lot of negotiations, he got me off with two years of probation, and $300,000 in restitution. The amazing thing is, I was put on a payment plan of 10% of whatever I earned in a month and I could definitely handle that. Then Jeff got busy trying to reverse my two-year probation.

Chapter Ten
"Pain"

*"My Heart Was Taken By You, Broken By You
And Now in Pieces Because of You" Unknown 12*

In December of 2010, Hermes was finally released from prison in Ecuador, but friends told me he was not the Hermes that I knew. Apparently, he had lost his mind, and was drinking and smoking weed. Friends said that everyday he was high as a kite, and waving guns all around, threatening to shoot somebody! What had happened to my baby? He even called Jason and told him that if I spent any time in jail he would put him in the ground! Hermes had clearly lost it and I couldn't get to him. It was driving me mad not being able to talk to him. I tried, but I could never reach him. He had moved and no one knew where he lived.

One day I decided to get online and look at his son's social media page. Maybe there was something there that could lead me to where Hermes lived. Looking at the page, I was stunned when I saw a message from a woman who said she was Hermes's wife and she posted their new phone number. I felt like somebody had thrown ice-cold water on me. I could barely breathe. My precious Hermes had married somebody else? I loosed my collar and I stretched out on the couch, trying to keep from passing out. For years, Hermes had been the center of my world. He dictated the direction of my life and I couldn't imagine living without him.

It was weeks before I got up the nerve to call Hermes's house. I dialed the number and heard his rich, mellow voice answer,

"Hello?"

"Hello, Hermes".

Clearly surprised, he answered, "How did you get this number? Uh, let me call you back."

And that was that. I hung up the phone, and cried my eyes out! What was happening?

Now I knew Hermes could contact me, so I waited. I was sure he would call and a month later, he did. The conversation was strained, as he asked me questions about my case. I did my best to stay calm, but it was hard to act like I wasn't upset about his new woman. I had to keep my cool, because I didn't want to scare him off. Finally, the conversation lightened and Hermes said he had a lot of things he needed to tell me. When he asked if I could travel to the Dominican Republic, my spirit soared! After the conversation, I got busy talking to Jeff about helping me get out of the country. Finally, after going back and forth he got me permission to go. Hermes wanted me to come on November 27th, right before Thanksgiving and he promised to wire me the money. He never did, and from the point on Hermes's number was disconnected and I didn't hear from him.

Time to Get Moving

Tax season was coming and I knew I could generate enough income to get things geared up. Since I didn't make my Thanksgiving trip the court gave me permission to go to the Dominican Republic to get my things. When I left the Dominican, I thought I would only be gone a few months so I left most of my things with Hermes. Clearly, Hermes and I weren't together anymore so I needed to get my stuff, and bring them back to the states.

On the way to the Dominican, I made a stop in Miami to visit Hermes's family. There were having a big event and I thought it was a good time to visit. I stayed with his family the entire time and we had a ball! Hermes's family is huge and we've always been really close. They loved me so much and I always felt like part of the family. After seeing everyone, it was time to go and I headed to the airport realizing that my real reason for going to the Dominican was to see about Hermes. I needed to get my clothes and other things, but the real driving force for my visit was to find out what was really going on with him.

During the time that I was going through all my court battles, I reconnected with my old friend, Veronica.

She's the one whose husband had been incarcerated with Hermes and we traveled to the prison together. When her husband Foster was released, she went to live with him in the Dominican. I emailed her and told her I was coming to get my things and she called me. It was so good to hear from her and we decided to meet for dinner that Friday. Later, she called me back and said that Foster wanted to go to dinner with us. I knew then that Hermes would definitely know I was in town.

When I arrived, I called Hermes's old assistant Jack, and told him I needed a driver. I kind of hoped he would also tell Hermes I was in town. When I got there I stayed at a hotel, and prepared for dinner with Foster and Veronica. It was good to be back in the Dominican. It's so beautiful! I had always loved the environment, the people, the food, and the nightlife.

That evening, I met Foster and Veronica for dinner and we had a really good time. It was so much fun talking about the old days, and catching up on the new things happening with each of us. I was blown away, when after dinner Foster and Veronica invited me to stay with them. I was so elated, because they were like family to me.

I was having a wonderful time until one day Foster moved in close and whispered, "If you're scared of sleeping in the guest room, feel free to get in bed with me and Veronica." I could hear the sexual undertones in his voice and I thought, "My God, are they swingers?" I was never into that whole swapping thing and I could never understand why anyone would want to share mates? To me, sex was an intimate thing, and should be kept private. As diplomatically as I could, I told him, "Thank you, but I'm very comfortable in the guest room". After asking me again on three separate occasions, Foster got the message. Thankfully, he didn't push it any further and they both continued to treat me really well.

One day, Hermes' driver Jack called and told me that he talked to Hermes. Now, here's the thing. Even though I never brought him up, no matter where I was or what I was doing, Hermes was always on my mind, so when Jack mentioned his name, everything in me lit on fire! When he finished speaking, my stomach felt sick and I could have thrown up all over the floor. Apparently Hermes told Jack, "Burn all of Cynthia's stuff! I'm not giving her shit!" I couldn't believe it and I was devastated! How could he treat me like that? I still loved Hermes and in my mind, he was still my man. If I hadn't figured it out before, now I was sure. It was time to move on, but how?

An old friend named Mike was in the Dominican and he gave Veronica and me tickets to the Cassandra Awards, which is the Latin version of the Grammy's. We went and felt like stars that night, walking the red carpet, and socializing with Latin celebrities. For the first time after I found out Hermes was done with me, I had fun. I met a lot of Latin stars and danced salsa at the after party. It was a magical night and Mike who escorted us, came on to me and with no hesitation, I responded. After that, Mike and I started dating. The funny thing is, Mike was Foster's friend, but Foster didn't mind. He knew that Hermes had moved on.

I really wanted it to work out with Mike, but in all areas that mattered, Mike was not Hermes. Hermes was strong and domineering, but Mike was just the opposite and in a few weeks the relationship was over. Mike just wasn't Hermes.

It was finally time for me to fly back to Cleveland and I felt empty. I salvaged whatever clothes I could and I left the rest. I just didn't have anymore fight in me. It was over and I had to move on. When I said my goodbyes to Foster and Veronica, I knew that the Dominican I had experienced from my time with Hermes, was for me totally different now. The magic was gone and now it was time to deal with the pain.

As I headed for the airport I felt cold and hollow, as if someone had sucked my insides out, leaving me with nothing, but an empty shell. When I arrived, I went through motions, trying to smile and be cordial, but it was hard, because I felt like a zombie...devoid of life.

When the flight attendant finally called for boarding, I shuffled my way to the plane and finally got off my feet that could barely hold me up. After the boarding chaos and the numbing safety demonstrations, the plane finally took off and I had time to think.

Looking back, I realized that if I had given up my citizenship and stayed with Hermes, we would probably have stayed together, or maybe we wouldn't. I didn't know, but I did know that during that time I couldn't defect from the United States. Everything and everyone I knew, was in Cleveland. To give it all up for Hermes was too hard.

When I left to deal with the allegations, I had no idea that it would be years before I returned to the Dominican. If I had known I would end up doing jail time and losing the love of my life, I might have made different choices, or maybe not. I didn't know. It was my crossroads experience. Now, it was all hindsight. What was done was done. I couldn't go back. I had to live with my choices. Exhausted, I laid my seat back, and drifted off to sleep.

The stewardess startled me, as she announced our arrival into JFK Airport. I must have been really exhausted, because I slept through the entire flight. I looked out the window at the New York skyscrapers and thought, "What a great country we live in". For a minute I had forgotten about Hermes and the Dominican, then the thoughts rushed in, hitting me in the stomach like a sucker punch! Through the pain I asked myself, "Did I make the right decision? Can I go on without Hermes?"

The stewardess told me to lift my seat in the upright position and make sure my seatbelt was fastened. As weak and vulnerable as I was, I appreciated the attention. I sat up and looked out the window again, as the thoughts of Hermes floated into my head. I started to remember the good times. I could feel the cold, porcelain toilet seat, as I remembered how Hermes would ask me to sit on the toilet and take notes while he gave me instructions for the day. The thought of it, made me chuckle. I remembered the Sunday morning drives along the ocean, and brunch at our favorite bistro. I always loved the walks with our dogs on Hermes' vast estate. My mind was reeling as I thought of our lovemaking, the laughter, and tears. I had to stop thinking. I could've easily driven myself mad. The only truth that I had to cling to was that it was over. I could have done a million different things, but I had decided to go home.

If you were in my shoes what would you have done? Or better still, when your crossroads experience comes, and it will, what will you do?

"Watch your step", the stewardess admonished us as we walked out of the plane and I thought to myself, "I certainly will."

To Be Continued…

SOURCES CITED

1 Maya Angelou." BrainyQuote.com. Xplore Inc, 2015. 30 May 2015.
http://www.brainyquote.com/quotes/quotes/m/mayaangelo101310.html

2 Soulja, Sister. Midnight: A Gangster Love Story. New York:
Washington Square Press/Simon & Schuster, 2008. Print.

3 Maze. Joy and Pain Album. Produced by Frankie Beverly On
Capital Records. 1980.

4 Floyd, Ruth Naomi. Ella Fitzgerald – "It Isn't Where You Came From,
It's Where You're Going That Counts." Web. February 17, 2013.

5 Cicero, Marcus Tullius. (n.d.). BrainyQuote.com. Retrieved May 30, 2015,
from http://www.brainyquote.com/quotes/quotes/m/marcustull118176.html

6 Brooks, Gwendolyn. BrainyQuote.com. Xplore Inc, 2015. 30 May 2015.
http://www.brainyquote.com/quotes/authors/g/gwendolyn_brooks.html

7 Gibran, Khalil. BrainyQuote.com. Xplore Inc, 2015. 30 May 2015.
http://www.brainyquote.com/quotes/quotes/k/khalilgibr136981.html

8 Maya Angelou." BrainyQuote.com. Xplore Inc, 2015. 30 May 2015.
http://www.brainyquote.com/quotes/quotes/m/mayaangelo101310.html

9 Vivian Greene. Viviangreene.org/learning-to-dance-in-the-rain/

10 Aberjhani. Christmas When Music Almost Killed the World. lulu.com;
1st edition. October 21, 2008.

11 Angelou, Maya. I Know Why the Caged Bird Sings. Ballantine Books;
Reissue edition. 2009. Print.

12 Unknown. Web. http://www.bestofquotes.org/my-heart-was-taken-by-you/

www.ingramcontent.com/pod-product-compliance
Lightning Source LLC
Chambersburg PA
CBHW050405030726
47503CB00006B/2032